Lock Down Publications and Ca$h Presents

I0658356

LOVE ME OR LET ME GO

WHEN FOREVER GETS UGLY

Written By
R. FACEY

First Edition 2025

Printed in the United States of America

This is a work of fiction. Names, characters, places, and incidents either
are products of the author's imagination or are used fictitiously. Any
similarity to actual events or locales or persons, living or dead, is
entirely coincidental.

Lock Down Publications
P.O. Box 944
Stockbridge, GA 30281
www.lockdownpublications.com

Like our page on Facebook: Lock Down Publications
www.facebook.com/lockdownpublications.ldp

Stay Connected with Us!

Text **LOCKDOWN** to 22828 to stay up-to-date with new
releases, sneak peaks, contests and more...

Like our page on Facebook:
Lock Down Publications

Join Lock Down Publications/The New Era Reading Group

Visit our website:
www.lockdownpublications.com

Follow us on Instagram:
Lock Down Publications

Email Us: We want to hear from you!

Acknowledgements

Yes, I'm back with another juicy story and I must say, I enjoyed writing this one. Big thanks to the Intel and Ms. Palode for costing me that well-needed 40 days in isolation to birth this work of art. It gave being an author under Lockdown Publications a literal meaning.

Thank you to my test readers, Mittens and Chez and my little promoters too. Once they found out I was an author, they told everybody like I was some kind of celebrity. I appreciate y'all for that.

Thank you to my publisher, Cash, for his patience during my transition from trial and freedom to prison and finding my groove again. Thank you for signing me and believing in me enough to add me to a group of talented authors including my best friend, DG Santana, my everything, my motivation, my drive. I appreciate and adore you for everything you are.

To my mother, for being the surest part of this prison experience. To God, most of all, for the blessing of creativity, for the constant and upcoming lessons in life, and for the reminder that vengeance is Yours, and to not conform to the ways of this world, like Romans 12:2 says.

And an extra shoutout to Mittens, you know why. This book wouldn't be here without you, girl.

Thank you.

Prologue

There's a certain kind of lonely that hits different at three something in the morning.

The kind that makes you double back on your healing.

The kind that whispers slick like:

You know exactly where you wanna be.

That was me.

Fresh out the shower again, the second one of the night, shaving shit that didn't need shaving, shea buttered up like I was prepping for a man who actually deserved me.

I threw on a red lace set.

Covered it with a muumuu, easy to slip off . . . since clearly I ain't learned shit.

I was listening to the demon on my right shoulder

"Pull up in thirty minutes."

Not a question.

Not a discussion.

A demand. And I listened like he still owned me.

And that's the crazy part....

I had just come from being turned down by the man who actually treat me like I matter.

Tool told me no earlier.

Not on some disrespectful shit…

but because I still legally belonged to the person I was headed to fall weak for.

I wasn't used to a nigga caring about my soul like that.

Sacave?

He never gave a fuck about the soul part.

Just the access.

We're in two different worlds…

and I picked the familiar one that hurt.

I looked at myself in the mirror, knowing I was trippin'.

Knowing this was a step backwards.

Knowing I was the reason my healing had potholes.

But I still grabbed my keys.

Still walked out.

Still drove like my feelings was in the passenger seat leading the way.

Every stoplight was a sign for me to turn around.

None of them mattered.

By the time I pulled up, I could see the light in the bedroom on like he was in there, preparing for me.

I went to call him then he opened the door. He smirked first. A smirk that basically said he won.

And the worst part?

He was right.

I wasn't here for love though.

Or respect.

I was here to feel wanted.

Just wanted.

I wasn't here for forever.

Forever got ugly.

Chapter 1

By the power vested in me, I now pronounce you man and wife. You may salute your bride.

On October 4, 2024, I married the best man I've ever experienced in my life. I was convinced after all the fuck niggas I ever had, I finally found love—like real soulful love, from the way he fucked me to the way he kissed me, his attentiveness, just everything unexplainable. He loved my son, Saviour, like his own. Saviour adored his biological dad, Sacavè, but he had just as much admiration for my husband.

But I'm getting ahead of myself. To understand how we got here, I need to take you back to the beginning . . .

I met my fine-ass 6'3" chocolate man at the QuikTrip, pumping gas into his candy-apple-red Chevrolet Silverado 2500 that he had so lifted you had to climb up in there. He had on a fitted white tee that was stretched tight across his frame, Nike fleece shorts, and some Nike slides. I was walking in for a slushie when he stopped me with the only lie he had ever told me:

"Aye, we went to school together. Yo fine ass done grew up."

I stopped in my tracks and looked at him real good. This man was fine as hell, but I couldn't place his face for nothing. I went to a big high school, but somebody looking like that? I would've remembered. Still, I played along because, honestly, I wanted an excuse to keep looking at him.

"Oh yeah? What year you graduate?" I asked, testing him.

He fumbled before he laughed and put his hands up.

"A'ight, a'ight, you got me. We didn't go to school together. But I had to say something to get you to stop."

Looking back now, I should've known right then that a man who opens with a lie that smooth was either trouble or the one.

We leaned up against his truck and talked and laughed until night broke. He told me about his job, how he had just gotten that truck lifted the way he wanted it. I told him about Saviour. He asked questions about him.

"How old is he? What's he into? He play any sports?"

Real questions, not the fake polite kind you ask when you're just waiting for your turn to talk.

We talked about everything and nothing. He made me laugh so hard my stomach hurt then he told me about his mama catching him and his sister as kids trying to cook

10

breakfast for her on Mother's Day and nearly burning the house down. I told him about the time Saviour convinced his whole kindergarten class that we had a pet tiger, and I had to go to school and explain that there was no such thing.

The sun had set and the parking lot lights had come on by the time I realized we'd been standing there for hours. My rest of my slushie had melted into a cup of colored sugar water that I had been holding the whole time. You would've thought we were old friends catching up. Before we parted ways, he said, "So you gone give me your number 'cause I'm gone give you my last name."

I laughed so hard. I found it funny for two reasons: one, I still have my baby daddy's last name that I waited 10 years for, and two, I never had a man so straightforward about something like that. Most men these days wanna "see where things go" and "not put a label on it" and all that other commitment-phobic bullshit. But here this man was, knowing me for a couple hours, talking about last names. Of course, I gave him my number, and the rest was history.

He texted, "Good morning, beautiful, have a good day" every day. Every single day. Even on the mornings when I knew he had to be up at 5 AM for work, that text would come through like clockwork at 6:30, right when my alarm went off. But between waking up every morning, getting me and

11

Saviour ready for the day; me for work and Savy for school, fighting with him about why he couldn't wear certain shit, packing lunch, finding matching socks, and all the other chaos that came with the territory. I never got around to replying to his morning messages.

But I would catch the one around lunchtime where he would say, "Lunch? I can't stop thinking about you."

I brought lunch to work every day, so I had to always turn down lunch. But the nigga was persistent. Every day, same question. "Lunch?" Sometimes he'd switch it up: "Let me take you to lunch." "You gotta eat, let me feed you." "I know you brought food, but my company is better than that Tupperware."

It just so happened that on Friday, Saviour gave me the hardest time waking up and getting ready. He was in one of those moods where everything was wrong his shirt was too itchy, his shoes were too tight, he didn't want cereal, he wanted pancakes but when I offered to make pancakes, he didn't want those either. By the time I had wrestled him into his clothes and given up on his hair looking presentable, we were running late. I had to call his father, and in the chaos of getting Savy out the door to meet Sacavè, neither of us got packed lunch.

Saviour actually played hooky with his dad. Sacavè texted me around 9 AM saying Savy had begged to spend the day with him and he'd already called the school. Fine by me. That extended his weekend trip by a day. So when lunchtime rolled around and my stomach was growling, that text came through. I finally said yes.

He picked me up from work in that big-ass truck. We ended up at Subway because I only had an hour. But he made a Subway sandwich feel like fine dining.

We sat on the back of his truck in the parking lot, feet dangling, eating our sandwiches and talking like we had all the time in the world. Sweet onion teriyaki sauce got on my shirt, but he just laughed and handed me napkins, saying, "That's how you know the food was good."

He asked me more about Saviour. He asked about Sacavè too, which surprised me. Most men don't wanna hear about your baby daddy. But he asked real questions. "Y'all cool? He treat Savy right? He take care of his responsibilities?" When I told him yes, that Sacavè was a good father although we didn't work out as a couple, he nodded like that mattered to him. Like he was taking notes.

Our lunch break went over, and I had to lie on Saviour's name for a family emergency when I got back. My supervisor gave me that look like he knew I was lying but

13

didn't push the issue. Thankfully, it was a down day at work and I didn't miss much. But I spent the rest of the afternoon with butterflies in my stomach, checking my phone like a teenager, waiting for his next text.

It came right as I was clocking out.

"Can I have you for dinner?"

The way he said it made my mind go everywhere, especially with Savy gone to Sacavè's for the weekend. My mind went straight to the gutter, I'm not even gonna lie. Of course, I replied.

"Have me?" I texted back, with the smirking emoji and everything. I was hot and ready like Little Caesars pizza, baby. There was no time limit for the right nigga, and I was ready, but he wasn't that type.

The nigga said, "Yes, be ready at 7:30. I'll pick you up."

He meant an actual dinner. A date.

On second thought, I'll be dessert. I agreed and sent my address.

I spent the next two and a half hours going through my closet. Everything was suddenly wrong. Too casual. Too dressy. Too tight. Too loose. Showed too much. Didn't show enough. I finally settled on a black dress that hugged me in all the right places.

I was putting on my lipstick, the finishing touch, when I got a notification on my phone about movement in my driveway. It was 7:28 PM.

That man was outside, standing next to his truck, and both him and that Silverado looked freshly washed and waxed. He had a fresh lineup, slacks that fit him perfectly, and a button-down with the first three buttons open, showing just enough chest. And in his hands? Two dozen red roses in a bouquet wrapped with Chanel gift paper.

This shit was new to me, no lie. My standards were in hell; Sacavè had set that bar so low. So, seeing this man I had known for all of a week, standing in my driveway looking like a whole Black romance novel cover? I wanted to be his appetizer, but I also wanted more than that. I wanted to take my time with this. I just know this man's daddy had to raise him right.

Our first date at *Knife* was nothing short of amazing. I wanted to be toxic about the fact that he knew the menu all too well, but he said he wanted me to experience his favorite restaurant with him. I'm a great mom, believe me, but I ignored Sacavè's calls all night. Whatever he wanted, as Saviour's father, he was capable of handling. I enjoyed my night.

Chapter 2

Sacavè didn't want shit. He called me to tell me that Saviour wouldn't eat his food. Fifteen missed calls, back to back, like our son was in the emergency room or had gotten hurt or something actually serious. But no. The nigga was calling about dinner. About mac and cheese and chicken tenders. About a meal that a grown man with a whole son couldn't figure out how to handle without blowing up my phone like the world was ending.

And when I finally told him why I didn't answer? That I was on a date, enjoying myself for once? I was everything in the book but a child of God. A hoe, selfish, trifling basically the whole dictionary of disrespect came at me through text messages.

I stayed on the phone with my new man as he drove home, listening to his voice. There was something peaceful about it. Something that felt right. When he got to his place, I was still on the line while he moved around, getting settled. I could hear him kicking off his shoes, the keys hitting the counter, him opening the fridge. Simple shit that felt intimate in a way I hadn't experienced in years.

I even stayed on while I showered, propping my phone up in the shower so we could keep talking about my job, about Saviour's obsession with Transformers, about my dreams of going back to school one day. He listened. Actually listened. Didn't interrupt, didn't try to one-up my stories with his own, didn't check out halfway through like Sacavè always did.

Meanwhile, Sacavè's texts kept lighting up my notifications like a slot machine. Each one angrier than the last. Each one more desperate. When I finally got out and checked, wrapped in my towel with water still dripping down my back, he'd sent me paragraphs about what kind of woman I was. I'm talking novel-length text messages about my character and my priorities.

This was all coming from a man that refused to sign divorce papers even though he was currently in a whole relationship with his side bitch bestie, the same bitch that was just his "best friend" when we were together, the one he swore I was tripping about. Meanwhile, this nigga was at her house every other day, helping her move furniture, bringing her soup when she was sick, texting her good morning before he even looked at me. And now he had the nerve to be in a full relationship with her while keeping me legally tied to him. Usher's "Papers" was the soundtrack of our whole situation.

I'm   ready   to   sign   them   papers,   papers,   papers
I done took all I can take but you leave me no options.

I love Saviour down, but having a baby with Sacavè was the worst decision I ever made. Not my son, never my son. Saviour is the best thing that ever happened to me. But choosing Sacavè to be his father? That was the mistake that would follow me for the rest of my life. It's that sick feeling of looking at your beautiful child and wishing to God you'd chosen a different father for him.

I continued to ignore calls from Sacavè while me and my new man talked about everything under the sun: his family, dreams, what we wanted out of life, where we saw ourselves in five years, our favorite foods, the music we grew up on. The conversation flowed so easily, so naturally like we had all the time in the world. I was sprawled out across my bed in my robe, phone propped up on my pillow, grinning so hard. This is what it was supposed to feel like. Light. Free. Uncomplicated. Not the weight I'd carried for years with

Sacavè with the constant pressure, the emotional drag, the feeling of being stuck in quicksand.

Then Sacavè's texts got more aggressive, more personal, more cruel. "It's you putting a nigga before your child, dumbass," popped up on my screen. Bitter ass nigga. I was too busy on cloud nine to entertain his kindergarten insults. I simply texted back, "He knows how to call me on his iPad."

I had bought Saviour that iPad specifically so he could reach me anytime he needed to, without having to go through his father. Added my number, showed him how to use it. My baby knew how to get to me. A call from my son's iPad was the only thing that was going to interrupt me and my man, and sure enough, not even ten minutes later, it came.

Sacavè was such a manipulator. The thought of me moving on, of me being happy with someone else, of me giving another man the time and attention I used to give him bothered him more than anything.

"Hold on, boo, this is my son," I said to my new man.

"Handle your business," he said. No attitude. No sighing. No making me feel bad about it. Just . . . understanding.

As soon as I answered the FaceTime, it was Sacavè's face across the screen, not Saviour's. That smug ass look he always had when he thought he was about to ruin my day with his twisted into this satisfied smirk. I had no tolerance left. I was disgusted with a man I once loved, a man I had given years of my life to, a man I had tried everything to make happy.

"Put my son on the screen or I'm hanging up," I said. I wasn't about to give him the satisfaction of an argument.

He instantly handed the iPad over to Saviour, but not before I saw him lean down and whisper something in my baby's ear.

"Mommy, can you come get me?" Saviour asked.

I vowed to my son that those words alone would always make me come running, wherever he was, whenever he called. It didn't matter what I was doing, who I was with, what time it was "come get me" meant I was on my way.

"Okay, son, what's wrong?" I asked, already standing up from my bed, looking for my keys, trying to remember where I had thrown my purse when I got home from the date.

I could hear Sacavè in the background, his voice low but clear enough for me to catch every manipulative word coaching my baby. Using him as a weapon in whatever sick game he was playing tonight. Sick son of a bitch.

"Nothing, Mommy, I just miss you," Saviour answered, and I could tell from the way his eyes shifted to the left.

Of course, those words hit me right in the chest anyway. What mother can resist "I miss you" from her baby? Even knowing Sacavè was pulling strings behind the scenes, even knowing this was a setup, my mama heart still ached. I was already grabbing my purse, slipping on my slides, ready to walk out the door in my robe if I had to. But something told me to ask more questions just in case I needed to gear up and show Sacavè and his bitch my daddy's daughter the side of me that don't play about my son, the side that would burn down the whole city if somebody hurt my baby. There had to be a reason he wanted my baby gone and I was gonna figure it out.

"I miss you more, baby. But is anyone making you uncomfortable? Is everything okay there?" I asked, looking for any sign of real fear, real distress, real need.

"No, Mommy," he answered faster than Sacavè could coach and I could see it in his eyes he was fine. He wasn't scared, wasn't hurt, wasn't in danger. He was just being used as a pawn in his daddy's petty games.

Regardless of the sorry-ass husband Sacavè was, he was a better daddy, and I told myself no amount of ill feelings towards Saviour's father would allow me to let that hinder their relationship. That was my promise to Saviour from day one. Whatever happened between me and his father stayed between us. My baby would never suffer because of our bullshit. We forcefully made our relationship work for the first three years of Saviour being born, barely speaking unless it was about the baby, living like hostile roommates in the same house. I left him on Saviour's fourth birthday and didn't look back.

Since then, I had texted niggas here and there, entertained a few phone calls, went on a couple dates, but nothing too serious. Nothing that made me feel anything. Nothing I had to bring around my son or let interrupt my peace. I think my new man intimidated Sacavè. This nigga heard the word "date" and went berserk, like the concept of me actually moving on, actually being happy with someone else, was impossible to process.

"He wanna spend time with his mama, that's why!" Sacavè chimed in, trying to narrate the situation.

"I'm on my way," was all I said before hanging up.

I jumped in my truck to go get my son before my future ex-husband started feeding him untrue bullshit, planting seeds in his head about his mama choosing men over him. I called my new man as I was backing out of the driveway.

"Everything good?" he asked.

"His dad on some bullshit, but I'm going to get him now. I'll call you when I get back," I said, frustrated.

"You want me to come with you? I can meet you there," he offered, and God, that almost broke me. Nobody had ever offered to step into my bullshit before.

"Nah, I got it. But thank you. I really appreciate that," I said, and I meant it.

"A'ight. Text me when you get there safe. And when you get back home. I'm up," he said.

Between hanging up and getting to Sacavè's house was 28 literal minutes. Twenty-eight minutes of driving through Atlanta at night, trying not to cry from frustration, trying not to let Sacavè win by pissin' me off. Twenty-eight minutes of wondering if co-parenting would get worse.

My son was asleep by the time I got there. My baby was cozy in his pajamas, cozy in his bed, completely knocked out. Mouth open, little snores, one arm hanging off the side of the bed. Peaceful. Unbothered.

"He's asleep now," Sacavè said, like that was supposed to mean something. Like that changed the fact that he'd just made me drive across town.

"So I can take him home," I said, trying to move past him into Saviour's room.

"He's comfortable now," he insisted standing in the doorway.

"I've carried him sleeping before Sacavè move," I demanded knowing I was capable of carrying him to car seat like I had done a million times before.

"You gon' struggle getting him out of the car seat at your spot. Just leave him, he's good here." He stressed with fake concern.

Absolutely the bullshit I deal with. The obstacles. The power plays.

To honor his dad's request and honestly, because I was tired of arguing, tired of standing in that doorway, tired of playing these games, I decided to stay and sleep in the bed with Saviour. Because I didn't want him to wake up feeling abandoned, feeling like mommy didn't come get him after he asked, feeling like his dad was right about me choosing other people over him.

"I'm staying then," I told Sacavè. "I'm sleeping in Saviour's room."

Sacavè looked surprised, like that wasn't the response he expected. "You can sleep in my room—"

"I'm sleeping with my son," I cut him off. "Since you won't let me take him home."

I climbed into Saviour's twin bed, my baby's little body curled up against me. At that moment, Sacavè won the battle, but he didn't win the war. Not even close.

Chapter 3

The next morning, me and Saviour woke up to breakfast in bed. His foot had been planted in my back since about 3 AM, which had become the new norm whenever we slept in the same bed. I slept in his twin bed twisted up like a pretzel trying to give my baby all the space he needed while I clung to the edge for dear life.

His full-of-shit daddy cooked eggs, pancakes, and sausages with a side of strawberries and grapes. Saviour's plate had a smiley face pancake, which I had to admit was the cutest thing: a pancake with whipped cream eyes and a chocolate chip smile. The presentation was impressive. When Sacavè dropped the plates off and walked back out without a word, I had to ask my son,

"Baby, does daddy always make you delicious breakfast like this?"

"Yes!" Saviour said excitedly, his mouth already full of pancakes.

It shocked me when he said yes. In all our years together, Sacavè had never cooked breakfast. Not once. Cereal was pushing it for him. But here he was, whipping up full spreads every weekend for our son.

It would surprise anyone to know me and Sacavè never fought in front of Saviour before, not once in almost five years. We kept our bullshit behind closed doors, in whispered arguments. Saviour was too young to eavesdrop on us. So, as irritated as I was, sitting in this house I used to call home, eating breakfast made by a man I couldn't stand anymore, I still put on a show for my baby.

"Hmm, this is delicious, thank you, daddy!" I said.

"I miss you calling me that," he responded with a big dumbass smirk on his face, walking back in with his own plate of food.

It put the biggest smile on my face when my son, completely oblivious to the tension, mocked me.

"Delicious! Thank you, daddy!" Saviour repeated, making both of us laugh.

It definitely lightened the moment Sacavè tried to create, this fake family breakfast scene. We sat like a happy family with Sacavè at the foot of Saviour's bed eating while me and Savy sat up top against the headboard, our plates balanced on our laps.

After we got done eating, I grabbed our plates to take them downstairs and wash them, walking through this house like it was still mine. Yes, the nigga kept the place that we lived in together. The house we'd picked out, the house we'd made a home. So much for a "real nigga." I got downstairs ready to wash the dishes and my whole mood shifted when I saw the kitchen. The only dishes to wash were the ones he'd transferred the food from IHOP containers into.

IHOP.

This nigga was over here conning my damn son into believing that he could cook. The evidence was right there. I should've known better because all those years we were together, I did all the cooking. Every single meal. Breakfast, lunch, dinner, and everything in between. I just assumed maybe Ms. BestieSideBitch had taught him something over time. Guess not.

I washed the dishes anyway shaking my head at the audacity. At the performance.

After I got done, it was about that time for me to leave because my days of playing house with Sacavè was over. I had to get back to my real life, back to my own space, back to reality. I walked upstairs to find them playing Madden. Well, Sacavè was playing Madden. My son was sitting next to him with a wireless controller that wasn't even turned on, mashing buttons and "playing" along, completely convinced he was controlling the game. Sacavè hadn't told him any different.

"Okay, son, you ready to go to Mommy's?" I asked, standing in the doorway with my purse already on my shoulder.

"Not yet, Mommy!" Saviour said without even looking away from the TV screen, his little thumbs still working that dead controller.

Sacavè laughed so hard you would think I had told a joke. He looked at me with this knowing smile, this "I got you" expression that irritated me more.

At this point, I knew I had to put my foot down with Saviour. Set a boundary. Make it clear.

"Saviour, when you go with your daddy, you're going to stay with your daddy. I love you, but I'm not coming to get you every time. You understand?"

"Yes," he said, still not really paying attention, still locked in on that screen.

"Sacavè, lemme talk to you real quick," I said.

"Ooooh!" Saviour instigated, finally looking up from the game with a mischievous grin.

I don't even know where he got that from. Kids pick up everything.

I gave my son a thousand kisses goodbye before I walked out of the room with Sacavè on my ass. I auto-started my car in the driveway before I even made it to the kitchen, so he knew this conversation was going to be quick. I hopped up on the kitchen counter and got straight to it.

"Sacavè, when are you gonna sign the divorce papers?" I asked, looking him dead in his eyes.

His whole face got sour real quick. The smile from upstairs disappeared. He thought he had me trapped, thought the breakfast and the laughs and the family moment meant something. The days of being gone over him were long over. I no longer cared for the last name I literally had to beg for, had to wait ten years to get. I'm cool with ex-wife, baby mama, "best you ever had" as my title at this point. I just wanted to be free.

"Why you in a rush all of a sudden?" he asked, fake busying himself in the kitchen, wiping down counters that were already clean, moving things around that didn't need to be moved.

You would think after making me wait ten years to give me his last name, it would be a breeze for him to let me drop it if I didn't want it anymore. Wrong. Dead wrong.

"I wouldn't say I'm in a rush," I said calmly. "But introducing you as 'my husband who's in a relationship with his bestie side bitch' is too much of a mouthful for me."

I was being petty about it, but who wouldn't be? This bitch was at my wedding. At my baby shower. She threw my baby shower. Hell, she's Saviour's godmother and now she's his stepmom. Sounds to me like they were fucking around this whole time and I was the only one who didn't know.

"You moved on . . . so what we talking about?" he asked, clearly fishing.

He wanted confirmation. Wanted details. Wanted to know about my date, about my new man, about whether I was serious or just entertaining somebody. But I'm not here to confirm or deny shit because I don't owe him anything but peaceful co-parenting.

"Which makes divorcing me easier, right?" I answered back, flipping his question.

Mind games used to work on me. His reactions, his jealousy, his possessiveness that shit used to do something to me back before. Made me feel wanted, desired, fought for. Not today. So when he stood there, shirtless, clenching his jaw, his ego clearly bruised, that shit didn't move me even the least bit.

"I'll sign them and get them and my requests over to my attorney this week," he said spitefully then started to walk toward the front door like he was ushering me out.

"What requests?" I asked, stopping in my tracks.

Fucking manipulator.

"You'll see when you get them. Kia, go ahead," he said, motioning toward the door with his hand.

This nigga didn't have any room for no muhfuckin' requests. When I left, the only thing I took was my son and the last name. I left the house, the truck he bought me, both rings on the kitchen counter, all the furniture, the dishes, the decorations, everything. I literally took my clothes, my son's clothes, and our personal items. That's it. He got everything else. And now he's talking about requests?

"Saviourrrr!" I yelled out toward his room.

"Kia, you not taking my son," Sacavè responded, stepping between me and the stairs.

"Nigga, I'm saying bye to my child. Cut the soap opera bullshit," I snapped. "And before you try to pull anything, remember your son is only a Sanders because we're married. You wasn't there to sign his birth certificate, so that's my son. I just let you borrow him from time to time."

Saviour came running down the stairs just in time to cut off whatever Sacavè was about to say. What a constant blessing my son was always showing up at exactly the right moment.

"Be a good boy for daddy. I'll see you tomorrow, okay, papa?" I said, kneeling down to his level, holding his little face in my hands.

"Yes, mommy," he answered back, wrapping his arms around my neck. "Love you!"

"I love you more," I said, squeezing him tight.

I love everything about being Saviour's mother. They say when your first child is a boy, it's because you need to feel true love. And I truly feel it every day. That unconditional, pure, nothing-like-it love.

"Kia, we need to get my name on his birth certificate," Sacavè said as I stood back up.

"WE don't need to do shit," I said. "I carried him for ten months. I pushed him out naturally. I named him. All you did was nut. You figure out how to get your name on your almost five-year-old's birth certificate now that I want a divorce. Move please, bookie."

Chapter 4

A text message from Tool read:

What's your favorite color?

Am I wrong for feeling like questions like this are so kindergarten? We been talking for a month now, been on multiple dates, stayed on the phone until 3 AM talking about everything under the sun, and now we're back to elementary school get-to-know-you questions? I thought.

"Pink," I texted back, answering anyway. Because even though it seemed simple, there was something about him wanting to know every little detail about me that felt different.

"So you mean to tell me I gotta wear pink at our wedding?" he texted back immediately, and I had to read it twice to make sure I saw what I saw. This man was different. Intentional. It had been a month now, and this was the third time he'd mentioned marrying me.

And honestly, I'm ready to see if Tool's dick is worth marrying, because Sacavè's dick was average. I just loved the nigga. That was the problem I loved him so much I convinced myself everything else was good enough when it wasn't.

"I gotta tell you something!" I texted back, anxious.

"Aw shit," he replied instantly.

I never felt like mentioning Saviour's dad being my husband was important because he's my soon-to-be ex-husband. I knew he needed to know, given that he'd mentioned marriage multiple times now. Honestly, I'm not interested in getting married and divorced a second time. Once was enough trauma for a lifetime.

"Tell me to my face," he said, double texting before I could even respond.

"My son is home," I texted back, which was true but also my excuse to not have this conversation right this second.

"If you don't want me to meet him yet, then come outside, bae," he texted back.

Before I could even type a response, I got a notification that there was movement in my driveway. This man was outside. I didn't even get a chance to get cute. I walked outside in my robe, hair in pin curls, raw and uncut at this point. Just me in my Thursday afternoon realness.

He was standing outside his truck with flowers. Pink flowers.

"These are so pretty! I have to get another vase. I still have the ones you gave me on Monday in the other," I said, smelling them.

I got flowers without even asking. Without dropping hints. I know I dealt with all kinds of sorry-ass niggas just to get to this moment. Just to experience what it felt like to be pursued.

"Pretty flowers for a pretty lady," he said, then smiled.

"Tevin, I—" I started to say, my voice serious now, ready to tell him about Sacavè.

"Wait, first name basis? You 'bout to break up with me already?" he cut me off.

Break up? I thought. *Wait. I have a boyfriend AND a husband? That's a lot going on. Too much going on.*

"I'm joking, lady," he said, laughing at what must've been the look on my face. he pulled me in for a hug fast then came with a forehead kiss.

Fuck.

There goes something reminding me of Sacavè. That was Sacavè's move. The way he used to calm me down. And now here was Tool doing the same thing, and I didn't know if I loved it or if it scared me.

Then, before I could process all that, out came Saviour, running out the door.

Like father, like son. Baby blocker.

"Truckkkkk! Hi! *Vroom vroom!*" Saviour said, his eyes wide, running straight past me to Tool's truck like it was the most exciting thing he had ever seen.

"Hey, you must be Saviour?" Tool said, kneeling down to his level. "You wanna drive?"

"Yesssss!" Saviour said, excited.

My heart dropped straight into my ass right then. *I can't—* I thought, frozen in place.

"Breathe, bae, everything cool," Tool said, looking back at me with those calm eyes. Like he could read my mind. Like he knew I was panicking.

I was stuck, flowers still in hand, watching him interact with Saviour's friendly ass so naturally. Like it was the easiest thing in the world. Tool lifted Saviour up into the driver's seat, and my baby was up there fake driving, hands on the steering wheel, making engine noises, having the absolute time of his life. Neither of them was paying me any mind. They were in their own little world.

"What's your name?" Saviour asked.

"Tevin. My friends call me Tool," Tool answered, adjusting Saviour so he could reach the wheel better.

"Tool!" Saviour repeated.

The interaction between them was so cute I wanted to cry. Saviour was usually standoffish and reserved like his dad, suspicious of new people, clingy to me around strangers. This was new. This was different. I loved every bit of it.

Until . . .

A tinted black BMW M6 pulled up to my house. Fast. Aggressive. The engine loud enough to make a statement.

Fucking Sacavè.

"Dadddddy!" Saviour yelled from his perch in Tool's truck, recognizing that car immediately.

Tool lifted Saviour from his truck carefully, setting him down so he could run and greet Sacavè, then looked back at me. His face was calm.

Sacavè hopped out with a Chick-fil-A bag, and Saviour ran into his arms like he always did. My baby loved his daddy, and I had never taken that away from him, but the timing of this was suspicious as fuck.

"Chick-fil-A!" Saviour yelled, reaching for the bag.

"Saviour, did you call your daddy for Chick-fil-A?" I asked, walking over.

I started grabbing the food out of Sacavè's hands like it was mine. I didn't know what to do with my hands, with my body, with this situation. My nerves just had me doing shit.

Then I set the bag on the back of Tool's truck because apparently, that made sense to my panicked brain.

"Yeah, he FaceTimed me and said he wanted crunch fries I don't know what that is, so I went safe and got Chick-fil-A," Sacavè answered, his eyes moving between me, Tool, and the pink flowers I was still holding.

"He calls Zaxby's fries crunch fries," I explained.

Tool was standing back, leaning on his truck ankles crossed and hands in his pockets. Calm. Collected. Like Sacavè had pulled up to his shit, not mine. I found that shit so sexy I had to look away before I started blushing.

"Yo man, I'm Tool," Tool said, walking up and extending his hand for a handshake.

"I'm Cavè. Her husband," Sacavè responded, gripping Tool's hand tight.

My mouth fucking dropped. My jaw literally fell open from shock that he'd just introduced himself as my husband to the man I'm dating when he knows damn well we've been separated, when he knows damn well he's with someone else, when he knows damn well he's only doing this to be petty.

"Cool, cool," Tool nodded, his face giving away absolutely nothing. Not intimidation, not anger, not insecurity. Nothing. Just cool acknowledgment.

When I say the way Tool kept his cool right there was so sexy. A man of restraint. A man who didn't feel the need to puff up his chest, mark territory or play games. He was secure. He was grown.

"Sacavè, please," I said, trying to cut through whatever weird alpha male energy he was trying to project.

I had to chime in because even though Tool was handling this perfectly, I wasn't about to let Sacavè embarrass me or disrespect him. This ain't that.

"Alright, K5, I'ma head out. Hit me up," Tool said, looking at me with soft eyes.

He had called me K5 because he said he'd heard of women with every car name, but never Kia. When he first said it, I had busted out laughing so hard you would've thought I was watching Kevin Hart stand up.

He gave me a side hug and another forehead kiss that made my pussy jump. That told me Sacavè introducing himself as my husband didn't make Tool feel threatened in the least bit. He wasn't competing. He was good.

"Okay, Tool Kit, and thank you for my flowers," I said.

"Anyway," Tool answered with a smirk, shaking his head at me.

He hopped in his truck and cranked it. The engine had this calm, sexy purr. That shit reminded me of him. Smooth. And to add insult to injury for Sacavè, Saviour mocked the sound as he and his daddy walked toward my garage door.

"Bye, Tool Kit!" Saviour yelled, waving with his whole arm. I smiled so big. Saviour was too good at this.

As soon as I walked inside, my phone dinged with a text message:

I enjoyed you and meeting your son, K5.

I was cheesing at my phone too hard and was about to text back when Sacavè had to ruin that moment too.

"That's why you want a divorce?" Sacavè asked, sounding bitter.

That man was on my ass even after introducing yourself as my husband. I thought. But I kept my response chill.

"No. I want a divorce because you're a terrible husband actually," I answered. "You all of a sudden want to introduce yourself as 'her husband' when you never wore your ring. You're sick."

This nigga had me in my own house, in my own space, feeling some type of way while he pushed my buttons in front of Saviour. But I'ma keep my cool though. I had to be the bigger person. For the sake of my son.

"Daddy, what's a *biborce*?" Saviour asked, his face scrunched up in confusion.

"A Porsche, son. It's a kind of truck," Sacavè said.

A lie was on that nigga's tongue so swift.

"Mommy getting a new truck?" Saviour asked, his eyes lighting up with excitement.

"Yes, baby, mommy wants a new truck. Mommy don't want the old truck no more," I answered back, playing along, turning Sacavè's lie into something that worked for me.

"Daddy, get mommy a *biborce?*" Saviour asked, so concerned, so sweet, so innocent.

"Exactly, son. Tell him!" I answered, pointing at Saviour like he was making the best point ever.

I was so excited that someone was encouraging this shit that I didn't care that it was a four-year-old who didn't know what was going on or what he was really saying. An ally is an ally.

"I'm not signing shit, K5," Sacavè mumbled under his breath, low enough that Saviour couldn't hear but loud enough for me to catch it. Then he laughed. "Daddy's going back to work, son. I love you!"

"I love you too, daddy! Come back with a *biborce*, okay?" Saviour responded, hugging his father's leg.

One thing about kids if they know you find something funny, they drill it into the ground until it's not funny anymore. I almost high-fived my child right there, but honestly, I had to work "biborce" out of his vocabulary before school tomorrow. I can't have him asking his teacher about divorces and Porsches.

I couldn't stop laughing though. And Sacavè hated it. Hated that I was unbothered. Hated that I was moving on. Hated that another man was in the picture. Hated that I was happy.

But that divorce was coming one way or another. Whether he signed those papers willingly or I dragged him through court, I was getting free. I had tasted what it felt like to be treated right, to be pursued. And I wasn't going back to settling.

Chapter 5

Ding.

As soon as I heard my doorbell ring, I checked the cameras on my phone to see who it was. Some petite white girl with blonde hair was standing at my door.

"Hey! I'm so sorry, I know you requested 'leave at the door,' but I tried messaging you in the app to say they didn't have the exact vase you requested. But if you don't like this one, I don't mind returning it and finding another," she said, all perky.

"Oh no, this is fine! My boyfriend must've ordered it. I didn't even know it was coming. But thank you so much," I said. "Hold on, let me get you a tip."

I pulled out a twenty, then thought about Tool's thoughtfulness. Fuck it. I grabbed five twenties instead.

"Oh my God, a hundred dollars? Thank you so much! Wow, thank you!" she said.

And this nigga Sacavè think being my husband gonna stop anything? Baby, please. Let me go snip and arrange these flowers so I can show my man what he did.

I spent the next twenty minutes arranging the pink roses in the new vase, taking pictures from different angles, making sure the lighting was right. Soon after, I texted Tool:

Thank you so much boo for the flowers and the vase.

His response was immediate:

You deserve it.

The next day came too fast. Morning routine with Saviour was always chaos. Today I had an extra mission. As I was packing his lunch and getting his backpack ready, I pulled him aside in the kitchen.

"Saviour, baby, remember what mommy said. No talking about trucks at school today, okay?" I said, getting down to his level.

"Okay mommy, no *biborce!*" he said with the biggest grin, then ran off laughing like it was the funniest inside joke in the world.

I couldn't do anything but put my hand over my face and shake my head. I really don't know how long I could keep "biborce" under wraps, honestly. I just didn't want his teachers treating any misbehaviors as divorce issues and calling me in for meetings, suggesting the school counselor, looking at my baby like he was damaged goods. Because if I didn't do anything else right in this situation, I was gonna make sure Saviour didn't feel our separation in a negative way. He had two parents who loved him. That was what mattered.

I dropped Saviour off at school, watched him run into the building with his *Transformers* book bag bouncing on his little shoulders, waved until he disappeared through the doors. Then I got back in my car and called Tool.

"Good morning, handsome," I said, pulling out of the school parking lot and heading toward the highway for work.

"Good morning, beautiful. What's going on with you?" he said, and I could hear the smile in his voice.

We talked and laughed all the way into work. Thirty-five minutes of conversation that felt like five. I was so into him telling me about his sister trying to set him up on a blind date before he met me that I had to hide my AirPods behind my hair when I got to the office and keep the conversation going.

I was at my desk, logging into my computer, pulling up my emails, when I knew I had to do it. Had to tell him. Had to get it out before I lost my nerve or before things got even more serious.

"So, remember what I said yesterday about having to tell you something?" I said, almost whispering.

"Yeah bae, what's up?" he said.

"I'm married."

The line got so quiet. I had to pull my phone out and look at the screen. Then I called his name.

"Tool?"

"Yeah," he said dryly.

Tool always had something to say, always had a comment, a joke. Until now.

But then he spoke.

"What else?"

He was straight-cut now, waiting for the rest of the story, for the full truth. I started stuttering.

"But we been separated for almost a year. He won't sign the divorce papers. We don't live together. We're not *together*-together. It's just . . . legally, on paper, I'm still—"

"Hmm," he made a sound.

I didn't know what that meant. I was ready to overanalyze.

"I'm not a husband or ever been one. But husbands? They lead with that. They stand on that shit with everything."

I ain't have shit to say. A man was talking, really talking, dropping wisdom, reading the situation better than I ever could, and I was mute. Listening. Absorbing. Learning.

He continued, his voice calm but firm. "For one, I wouldn't have so much of my time if you was happily married. Don't get me wrong, I'm a man of God, so I'm not fucking nobody's wife. But I can tell by yesterday he wasn't secure in his position or he didn't appreciate what he had when he had it. I actually thought he was joking."

I didn't want to act like I wasn't used to a man with sense, with discernment, with the ability to read a room and a situation. But Jesus Christ. That's what you call emotional intelligence. That's what you call a grown man who's done the self work. I was lost for words except for one.

"Amen," I whispered.

He continued, "He who finds a wife finds a good thing. What did I tell you when I asked for your number that first day at the QuikTrip?"

"That you were gonna give me your last name," I said.

"Did I sound unsure about that?" he asked.

"No," I responded.

"Huh?" he pressed.

"No, you sounded sure," I said.

When I say it felt like this man just fucked me so good? Like fucked me and talked me through it.

"Okay then," he said, like the conversation was settled.

All this time I literally begged for Sacavè's last name. Waited almost ten years for it. Cried over it. And here comes a man I've known barely over a month who just wants to give it to me.

"Tevin, why are you single?" I asked.

This was me trying to find something wrong, trying to locate the red flag, trying to figure out the catch. Because why is a man this attentive, this intentional, this fine, this accomplished, this communicative, with no kids, single? It didn't add up. There had to be something.

He was quiet for a second.

"I have terrible trust issues. I was with a woman for five years. She gave me two kids. I found out she cheated, so I left her. When she tried to put me on child support, that's when I found out they weren't mine."

"Wow," was all I could say.

"Yeah. So I stayed single for a couple years and did my young nigga shit clubs, different women. But I'm tired of that. I love coming home to one person," he said.

"I'm sorry about that. I know that has to be the worst feeling in the world," I responded.

"Back then, yeah. I'm cool now," he said, and I could hear the truth in it. He moved on.

I couldn't do shit but empathize. That was some tough shit to go through. But I also couldn't help but think from her perspective. I guess this is why they say never tell your next how your ex did you, because now I'm curious about his role in it. It's like reading a Yelp review on a nigga I just needed to know what his ex thought of him, what went wrong, where he fell short. I know no nigga is perfect, but I've been through enough bullshit to settle.

"Why do you think she cheated? Or why did she say she cheated?" I asked.

"I had just started my job, before I became supervisor. I was in grind mode, working overtime, doing everything to make sure the kids I thought were mine didn't need for shit. I didn't have the time I have now for dates and attention and all that.

I had to respect that answer. That was honest. That was self-aware. But it's called balance, and I wouldn't say his ex was wrong for wanting more time and attention. But I was raised being told that people make time for what they want to, so I wanted to understand.

"What's the difference now?" I asked.

"I'm a supervisor with no kids," he said. "I got time now. I got resources now. I got wisdom now. I'm not that same nigga no more."

49

I felt like a giddy little girl. This man was so fucking charming.

"Hmm, well, congrats on your new position then," I answered back, trying to sound casual when really I wanted to scream into the phone about how perfect he seemed.

"'Preciate it, bae. But speaking of, I been ducked off talking to you. I gotta head into this team meeting, but I'ma call you back on my lunch, a'ight?" he said.

"Okay," I said, trying not to sound disappointed even though I was. I didn't want to be too clingy, but damn, I was loving this conversation and didn't want it to be cut short.

Either way, when we disconnected, I threw myself into work. Emails, reports, phone calls with clients, data entry keeping busy and making the time pass faster. And surprisingly, the workday flew by. It got so hectic that I couldn't even answer when Tool called me back during his lunch. By the time I looked at my phone, I had three missed calls from him and a text:

Damn, you working working today lol. Call me when you free.

We finally reconnected on my way home from work. The highway was packed, rush hour traffic barely moving, but I didn't even care because I had him in my ear.

"You had me worried, K5. Thought you was ignoring me after this morning," he said.

"Never that. Work just got crazy," I said, merging lanes.

"So what you got planned for the weekend?" he asked.

And that's when I remembered it was Friday. Sacavè had picked up Saviour straight from school for his weekend. It was a kid-free, wine-filled weekend. Just me and maybe time with Tool.

"Nothing," I said. "Saviour's with his dad for the weekend. I'm free."

The line went quiet for a second, and then Tool's voice came through, lower, more intentional.

"Oh yeah? You tryna see me then?"

I bit my lip, already feeling that slow pull he had on me even during a casual conversation.

I couldn't say no. I wanted to see him. Hear him. Feel him. Just be around a man who made me feel like I didn't have to beg for basic shit like effort and consistency.

So I smiled, easing back into my seat as the traffic inched forward.

"You know I do."

Chapter 6

"So what did he break that I gotta fix?" Tool asked.

I had just gotten home, barely had time to kick off my heels when Tool texted asking if I wanted to go take a walk in the park. Of course I agreed. Twenty minutes later, we were walking the trail at Piedmont. He was asking me questions while we walked and held hands like a happy couple. Everything about it felt so healthy.

"I wouldn't say it's something to fix," I started, choosing my words carefully. "But I'm not falling victim to history ever again. I won't stay around just because we have history or because of my love for a person. If it's not right, I'm still leaving."

I meant that shit too. Something about having a child, watching Saviour love me unconditionally with his whole heart even though he had no money, no power, no agenda, that taught me something. If a little person with nothing to offer but pure love can make me feel loved correctly, then a grown person with resources and choices damn sure should be able to. I wasn't settling anymore.

"I feel you on that. Same for me," he said. "I rather be alone than be with someone who don't appreciate what I bring to the table."

The mutual understanding was so necessary. It showed me we had both been victims of history, both been burned, both learned our lessons. And we weren't about to make those same mistakes again.

After that, he stopped walking, turned to face me, and picked me up with those big, tattooed, muscular arms, palming my ass, and planted the best kiss ever on me. I could've fucked him right there in the park, witnesses be damned, but instead, we took it back to his place.

His house was beautiful, a two-story, four-bedroom, two-and-a-half-bathroom house with a two-car garage in a nice quiet neighborhood. Inside felt like a real home, nicely decorated for a man's house. Not sterile and empty like most bachelor pads. He had furniture that matched, art on the walls, plants that were actually alive. He held me by my waist while he showed me around, sneaking neck kisses between each room.

"This yo' kitchen. You say you like islands? I got one. Fridge full, pots, pans, whatever. I want you to cook me your favorite meal here," he said as we stood in the kitchen with its granite countertops and stainless steel appliances. "But right now I wanna eat you."

It was after that declaration that he picked me up literally swept me off my feet and carried me to the master bedroom. He tossed me on his king-sized bed.

"This is our room," he said, looking down at me with intense eyes.

Our room. Not *his* room. *Our* room. Like he'd already decided this was permanent, that I belonged here with him.

He kissed me everywhere. And I mean *everywhere*. He left no body part unkissed my lips, my neck, my collarbone, my breasts, my stomach, my thighs, the inside of my wrists, behind my knees, my ankles. Every inch of me got his mouth's attention. Then he got to my clit, pulled that sensitive bundle into his mouth, and went to work like it was his job. Like he was getting paid to make me cum. Like my pleasure was his only mission.

I came so many times I didn't know I had that many orgasms in me in one setting. My legs were shaking, my voice was hoarse from moaning, my hands were gripping the sheets so hard I thought I would rip them. At that point, I was feening. I wanted to feel him inside of me, wanted to know what his dick felt like, wanted to give back what he had just given me.

But this man told me no.

"No?" I said, breathless, confused, reaching for his belt.

"I told you, I'm not fucking nobody's wife but my own. So handle that," he said, then kissed my pussy one more time, then my stomach, then my lips, tasting myself on his tongue. And then he got up. Just got up. Left me there, naked and satisfied but also frustrated as fuck.

"But I want to please you too," I whined, and I damn near whispered that shit. I was so weak, so desperate to give him what he had just given me.

That man had just sucked my soul and energy out of me, left me boneless on his bed. I wanted to reciprocate. Needed to.

"It pleased me to please you. I'm practicing semen retention. I'm cool," he said, adjusting himself in his shorts.

"Semen retention?" I said out loud, sitting up on my elbows. "You practicing semen retention?"

This man just turned down the best head he could've ever received from me for the lamest bullshit reason I had ever heard in my life.

"Well, you asked me what makes me feel unwanted. It's this. Rejection," I said.

The man went and got a hot rag from his bathroom, came back, and started wiping me down gently while looking at me like I was talking nonsense.

"Baby, you can't possibly feel rejected by me right now. I just kissed every part of your body. I just made you cum four times. You hear yourself?" he said.

He looked me in my eyes while he said every word, his hands still gentle as he cleaned me up.

"You just pleased me by doing that alone. It was my pleasure," he said.

I realized I liked his restraint until now. I know I had been attracted to his discipline, his control. But this one honestly didn't feel right. What man didn't like his dick sucked? What man turned down that type of pleasure?

"A man with sexual discipline," he said, answering me as if he'd heard me ask that question out loud.

As soon as he finished cleaning me up, folding the rag neatly and setting it aside, I jumped up, got myself dressed, grabbed my keys from where I had dropped them on his dresser, and left. Didn't say goodbye. Didn't explain. Just walked out of his house, got in my truck, and drove home.

I got home and jumped in the shower with the quickness. I felt dirty. Rejected. Confused. I still couldn't wrap my head around why Tool just wanted to eat me out with no pleasure in return. What kind of man does that? What was his angle? What was he trying to prove?

When I got out of the shower, wrapped in my towel, dripping water on my bathroom floor, I checked my phone. I had a couple of missed calls from Tool and a FaceTime from Saviour. Of course, I called my sunshine back first.

"Hey, Savy, what you doing?" I asked as soon as he answered.

"Hi, mommy!" he said, but I couldn't see his face. Just the ceiling of what looked like Sacavè's living room.

"You having fun with daddy?" I asked.

"Yes!" he said, still not showing me his face.

"Why can't I see your face, baby?" I asked.

Nine times out of ten, he was too busy playing *Roblox* to pay me any mind. My son was a gamer already at four years old.

"Yo, Kia, call my phone real quick," Sacavè said in the background.

He was always going to find a way to get some screen time with me, always had to insert himself.

"Okay, mommy's baby, call me later and tell me goodnight, okay?" I asked.

"Yes!" Saviour said, and before I could even get out the words "I love you," this boy hung up his iPad, forcing me to go ahead and call his annoying ass daddy.

I sighed, pulled up Sacavè's contact, and hit call.

"Yes, Sacavè?" I said, already annoyed.

"Damn, we can't talk no more?" he asked.

"Sacavè, talk fast. I gotta call coming in," I lied.

"Fuck that nigga," he responded immediately, and I could hear the jealousy, the bitterness, the possessiveness.

I already knew where this conversation was going, so I went ahead and hung up my phone. He didn't want shit, and I surely wasn't in the mood for casual conversation.

I binge-watched episodes of *Good Girls*, drank some *Taylor Port* straight from the bottle, didn't even bother with a glass, until I fell asleep on my couch, still wrapped in my towel, the TV still playing in the background.

Tool hadn't tried to call anymore since earlier. And honestly, it was whatever. I didn't lose shit. I guess now I can be even more relieved that I didn't put my mouth on him. Fuck him and his semen retention. That nigga left me horny like dick wasn't easy to get, like it wasn't just a phone call away.

So I started dialing.

It was 3 o'clock in the morning when Sacavè answered, his voice groggy and confused.

"Where my son?" I asked.

"Man, it's 3 o'clock in the morning. Where you think he at?" he said back, irritation in his voice.

"Lemme see him," I demanded, my voice leaving no room for argument.

Sacavè switched to FaceTime to honor my irrational request, and I watched the screen as he walked through his dark house to Saviour's room. The camera showed my baby sleeping peacefully, mouth open, arm hanging off the bed, completely knocked out.

"I'm not talking about my son, Sacavè," I said.

He flipped the camera so fast, and his face filled the screen, confused at first, then that cocky smile spread across his face.

"Man, Kia, what you on?" he asked, but he had a big-ass smile on his face like he knew exactly what time it was. Like he'd been waiting for this call. Like he knew I would come back eventually.

This was exactly the reaction I needed from a nigga when I'm willing to put the pussy on him.

"I want some," I said simply.

His face lit up brighter than a Christmas tree that smile got even bigger.

"Sena here," he said, referring side bitch bestie who was now apparently sleeping in what used to be my bed.

"You telling me you don't know how to get rid of that bitch, Sacavè?" I asked.

I know I sound fucked up right now. I know I'm being messy, being reckless, being everything I tell myself I'm not. But if you want to be technical? That's my husband. Legally, on paper, in the eyes of the law, that man is still mine. And I'm not wrong for wanting to fuck my husband.

"Pull up in thirty," he demanded.

That was like music to my ears.

I showered again, the second shower of the night, this time taking my time. Exfoliated. Shaved everything. Lotioned up with cocoa butter. Put on a red lace set from *Victoria's Secret* that I had. Threw a muumuu over it, nothing too fancy, just something easy to take off. Spritzed perfume on my neck, my wrists, between my breasts.

I knew this was wrong. Knew I was making a mistake. Knew I was about to do something I would regret. But right now, in this moment, I didn't care.

I just wanted to feel wanted. And Sacavè, for all his flaws, for all the ways he'd failed me as a husband, had always made me feel that in the bedroom.

***

I pulled up to Sacavè's house exactly thirty minutes later; my heart started beating fast. As soon as I put the truck in park, he opened the garage door.

He was shirtless, wearing nothing but grey sweatpants that hung low on his hips. Even from the driveway, I could see that look in his eyes, the one that used to make my knees weak back when shit was good between us.

"You really something else," he said as I walked up to him.

"You are too," I responded, my muumuu flowing around my legs in the night breeze.

He didn't say anything else. Just grabbed my hand and pulled me inside, closing the door behind us. The house was dark except for the dim light coming from upstairs.

"Where's Saviour?" I asked, suddenly remembering our son.

"Sleep. In his room. Door closed," Sacavè said, his hands already finding my waist, pulling me closer.

I could smell his cologne likely one that I bought. Like Creed or something. My body remembered him before my mind could catch up, responding to his touch in ways I wished it wouldn't.

"You wanna divorce everything but this dick?" he asked, his lips inches from mine.

I nodded.

He kissed me deep, familiar and possessive. His hands slid under my muumuu, finding the red lace underneath, and he groaned against my mouth.

"Fuck," he breathed. "You know lace make me weak."

He knew exactly how to touch me, how to kiss me, how to make me forget why I left in the first place.

He walked me backwards toward the stairs, our lips never breaking contact. We made it halfway up before he got impatient, pressing me against the wall, his hands everywhere my thighs, my ass, working the muumuu up and over my head. It fell somewhere on the steps behind us.

"Red too," he said, looking at me in nothing but the lace set. "My favorite color."

"I know," I whispered.

He picked me up, my legs wrapping around his waist automatically, muscle memory from years of this. He carried me the rest of the way up the stairs and into the bedroom, kicking the door closed behind us.

The room smelled different. Like perfume drowned out with air freshener. Like Sena had been here, in this bed, in this space that used to be mine. It should've stopped me. Should've made me turn around and leave.

But then Sacavè laid me down on the bed and started kissing down my neck, across my collarbone, between my breasts, and I stopped thinking about her. Stopped thinking about anything except the way his mouth felt on my skin.

"I missed this," he said against my stomach, his hands unhooking my bra with practiced ease. "Missed you."

My bra went somewhere on the floor. His mouth found my nipple, sucking, biting gently, making me arch off the bed. His hand slid between my thighs, over the lace of my panties, feeling how wet I already was.

"Damn, man," he groaned. "You know I missed this shit?"

I didn't answer. Couldn't. He hooked his fingers in the sides of my panties and pulled them down slowly, his eyes never leaving mine. Once they were off, he stood up and pulled his sweatpants down, no boxers underneath.

He was already hard, ready, and for a second I just stared regretting.

"Come here," I said, reaching for him.

He climbed onto the bed, settling between my legs then kissed me again, slower this time, like he was savoring it.

"You want this dick?" he asked one more time.

"Yes," I breathed. "I want it."

He slid inside me slowly, giving me time to adjust, to remember how we fit together. My nails dug into his back as he started moving, deep strokes that had me gasping his name.

"Fuck, Kia," he groaned in my ear. "You feel so good. So fucking good."

He knew exactly how I liked it, the pace, the angle, the way he'd pull almost all the way out before pushing back in. He knew how to make me fall apart.

"Right there," I moaned, my legs wrapping tighter around his waist. "Don't stop."

"I ain't stopping," he promised, his pace quickening. "This my pussy. Always been mine."

I came first, my whole body shaking, while I moaned his name. He followed right after, burying his face in my neck, his body tensing before he collapsed on top of me.

We lay there for a moment, both breathing hard, our bodies slick with sweat. Then he rolled off me, pulling me against his chest like he used to, like we hadn't spent the last year destroying each other.

"Stay," he whispered into my hair.

And against my better judgment, I did.

We went again an hour later. And then again after that, like we were trying to make up for lost time, like we could fuck our way back to when things were good.

By the time we finally fell asleep, tangled in sheets that smelled like sex and regret, the sun was starting to come up.

I didn't dream. I just fell into a deep, exhausted sleep in my husband's arms, knowing that when I woke up, I'd hate myself for this.

But that was tomorrow's problem.

Chapter 7

I hated confusing Saviour. He went to sleep with Sena there and woke up to me and Sacavè in bed with Sena gone. But I was too knocked out to get up and go lay in Saviour's bed like I should have. Instead, my baby ran into the room to see me sleeping in Sacavè's bed, demanding breakfast from his daddy like it was any other Saturday morning.

His voice woke me up. All I could manage was a groggy "Hey, mommy's Savy" as I tried to open my eyes and orient myself to where I was.

When I went to reach for him, to pull him into a hug, I realized my clothes were everywhere but where they needed to be and I was butt-ass naked under these sheets. Sick. I felt sick to my stomach.

I guess Saviour was too excited to see me to even focus on that detail. Too young to understand.

"Mommyyyy!" he said, climbing onto the bed.

Him calling out for me with everything made the shame start to settle in heavy. I had no business being naked in his father's bed, confusing him about what was going on. Honestly, confusing both of them, because I still wanted a divorce. This didn't change anything. And only God knows what Sacavè's lying ass had to say to Sena to get her to leave at three something in the morning, which further explained the sneaky-ass nigga he was.

I can't lie like he didn't fuck me good though. Shit was better than I remembered. Better than it had been when we were actually together. Maybe it was the desperation, the anger, the need to prove something. Whatever it was, three rounds later, we both passed out.

"Is there food in the fridge?" I asked, trying to shift into mom mode.

"Yeah, Sena went shopping yesterday," Sacavè said.

I rolled my eyes. That was easily a yes or no question, but he had to mention her name, had to remind me that she existed, that she'd easily comfortable, playing the role in his life.

"Take Saviour downstairs and take the breakfast stuff out. I'll cook," I said.

I really needed time alone while I put my clothes on. Needed a minute to collect myself. I know Sacavè felt my regret radiating off me. It was written all over my face.

"Mommy, you coming?" Saviour asked, pausing at the doorway.

"Yes, baby, go ahead and start getting the breakfast stuff out," I said, forcing a smile for my son.

As soon as they left the room, I jumped up, inched down the stairs to get my muumuu, splashed some water on my face in Sacavè's bathroom, and tried to pull myself together.

When I got downstairs, I looked around the kitchen and opened the fridge. Sacavè said Sena had gone shopping, but there absolutely was no breakfast food in here. No bacon, no pancake mix. Just eggs, leftovers, lunch meat, and random shit. But there were shrimp in the freezer.

I got to work making my infamous shrimp and grits with scrambled eggs, the meal I used to make every Sunday morning when we were a family, when things were good.

"I miss this shit, Kia," Sacavè said from where he was leaning against the counter, watching me cook in his kitchen like old times.

Here we go. I know he wasn't just talking about my shrimp and grits either. I knew better. So I'm going to have to take everything that comes with my impulsive sexual decisions. This was the consequence, him thinking this meant something, thinking we were back together, thinking three rounds of dick was enough to fix years of bullshit.

"Sacavè, don't start," I said, not looking at him, focused on stirring the grits so they wouldn't burn.

"I miss my family," he continued.

Now this nigga misses his family? When eight hours ago he had to kick his side bitch bestie out for me to come over? When he's been with Sena for almost a year, playing house with her? This shit was about to give me a headache.

"Savy, put your iPad down and eat your food, please, son," I said, needing to break the tension, needing something else to focus on besides Sacavè's puppy dog eyes.

"Yes, mommy," Saviour said, pausing his *Roblox* game reluctantly.

We all sat at the table together like a real family. The only sound was Saviour's paused *Roblox* music playing from his iPad because nobody said a word.

Sacavè scarfed his food down like he hadn't eaten in days, like this was the best meal he'd had in months. Saviour danced in his chair after every bite, then looked up at me with those big eyes.

"More please!" he said, holding up his plate.

"Of course, son," I said, my heart warming despite everything. Saviour was a picky eater, always had been. When he asked for more of home-cooked food, especially something with vegetables and protein, it was heartwarming.

"I'll get it, Kia. You finish eating," Sacavè chimed in, standing up from the table.

He got up with this sad, longing look on his face to make Saviour's second round, and it made me regret this even more. Made me feel like I had given him hope when there was none. When he came back with the plate, he slid something across the table toward me.

My second wedding ring. The one I had left on the kitchen counter when I moved out. The one I had told him to keep or throw away because I didn't want it anymore.

"Sacavè, stop," I said.

I had to get up from the table at that point. That was my cue to end this, to set shit straight, to make sure we never did this shit again. Because I had no desire to be with my baby daddy anymore. Last night was a mistake. This morning was a mistake. All of it was a fucking mistake.

"Saviour, take your iPad and go upstairs for a sec, baby," I said.

"Okay, mommy!" he said, grabbing his iPad and running upstairs, happy to get back to his game.

When Saviour was clear, I let Sacavè have it. Had to say what needed to be said, had to make this crystal clear.

"Sacavè, you fucked me so good. I mean, so good," I said, being honest, giving him that much. "Like, I'm not even gonna lie about that."

He moved closer, a smile spreading across his face, thinking I was about to say what he wanted to hear. He picked me up and sat me on the countertop like round four was about to happen right here in the kitchen.

"But not good enough to make me still want to be your wife," I finished, and I watched his face fall in real time.

Now that I think about it, did he even change the sheets from the ones Sena had been laying on?

He backed up like I had two heads, like he couldn't believe what was coming out of my mouth. Like he expected the complete opposite. He was one shallow ass nigga to believe it took three rounds of dick and eating my ass to get me back. To fix everything.

"Kia, stop playing with me," he said in that threatening tone, that possessive tone I used to think was sexy.

Him saying that shit and grabbing my waist used to turn me on at one point. Not no more.

"I'm not playing, Sacavè. On my son, I still want a divorce," I said.

When I put anything on Saviour Amir Sanders, I was dead serious, and he knew it too. That was my unbreakable vow. I never played about my son.

"Kia, you made me put this bitch out in the mid—" he started.

I cut him off before he could finish. "I didn't make you do anything. I asked to get fucked and you did what it took, I guess. But that's it. That's all this was."

He was shocked, genuinely lost for words that I was even talking to him like this. But yes, the tables had turned. The power dynamic had shifted.

"I cracked you like an egg, my boy. Appreciate that," I said, then jumped down off the countertop, ready to go home and forget this ever happened.

I was so amused that the ball was in my court for once, that I had the power, that I had gotten what I wanted and could walk away. Until he grabbed me by my neck, not choking me, but dominant, and stuck his tongue down my throat. Kissed me hard and possessive.

He held my face in both his hands and started talking between kisses. "You"—*peck*—"called"—*peck*—"me daddy"—*peck*—"and said that pussy"—*peck*—"was mine"—*peck*—"last night"—*peck*. "And I believe you. It felt the same since I last had it, so it's still mine, Kia."

"Nigga, I was drunk," I lied, pushing him away.

"I bet. Why you ain't call muscle man to come scratch that itch then?" he said back.

Muscle man was hilarious. Clearly, Tool was living rent-free in his head making him insecure.

""Cause my husband was easy," I said back with a shrug, like it was simple, like it didn't mean anything.

I mean, I didn't lie. He obviously wasn't easy, and Sacavè was, so I cracked him Sunnyside up.

I said my goodbyes to Saviour then sashayed my fast ass out the door. I drove home feeling regretful but satisfied. It felt like an ego thing like I still got it, although I opened a whole new can of worms with Sacavè making him feel like it meant something. I was worn out as I got home. I kept myself occupied cleaning up my home and doing mine and Saviour's laundry. I can't lie like those rounds didn't give me an extra pep in my step. I was spring cleaning in the Fall. Hours had wa passed with mot even a text or call and I didn't even care. He probably expected me to return his call from yesterday too, but what could he possibly be calling to say anyway? He didn't attempt to stop me when I was leaving his house. He watched me grab my keys, walked down some stairs, out the front door, down some more stairs and down the pathway to the driveway and enter my truck and drive off. If he was anything like Sacavè could've caught me before I went out the door. I finished cleaning, and ordered grocery delivery to replenish what we use that last week before running a bath. I climbed out of my muu muu smelling like Sacavè, a gagful reminder that I doubled backed on my baby daddy after over a year. I turned up my Bluetooth speaker for the music to drown out my thoughts as I climbed down and relaxed while Kehlani sang in the background.

**

"Amen!" I said, clapping as Pastor Lee spoke to preached like he was speaking directly to me that happened every time I hadn't been at church in a while and five years ago at one point, I was convinced that because my mama is apart of the church family that maybe she was telling him past my damn business. Something pulled me to church this morning, though it couldn't have been sin because I didn't commit none having sex with My Husband.

"Where's my grandson?" I heard my mama ask as I was walking out the door.

"At his dads mama," I said turning around and reaching to hug her.

She eyed me up and down eyes full of judgment and maybe shock.

"Hmm, next time wear a jacket over there," she said, pulling my dress down. " And maybe some stockings."

"Ma, this is not the modern days!" I said, turning on my heels. "I gotta go get your grandson and I'll call you."

With that, I walked off that's why I'm rarely here now. I don't want to have to squeeze into anyones standards. I want something I wore something I had worn to work before. If it wasn't inappropriate then it should be now. And honestly intended on getting Saviour this early, but I hadn't heard from him and was near Sacave's house anyway. When I pulled into his driveway, us fucking came back to mind making my pussy jump. Sick. Real sick. I walked up to the door my thoughts must've reached my expression because Sacavè opened it and I gave him a disgusted look, then pushed past him.

"Saviour! It's time to go baby!" I yelled.

"I coulda dropped him off," Sacavè added walking up behind me with lustful eyes.

I instantly rolled my eyes. "It's okay I was in the area."

I grabbed Saviour, got him in the car despite his protests about wanting to stay and play more, and drove home in silence.

When I pulled into my driveway, I saw a mini version of Tool's truck, red and black Power Wheels Silverado parked with a vase of pink flowers sitting in the passenger seat.

"Ooooh, mommy, look!" Saviour yelled from the backseat, practically climbing over his car seat to see better.

Saviour was so excited. He had many automatic cars, but this was his first truck. And it looked just like Tool's real truck.

I loved how thoughtful Tool was with both gestures, the flowers for me, the truck for my son. It made me feel worse for impulsively giving my baby daddy some pussy. But Tool was on ice regardless. He'd rejected me first. This was his fault, in a way. If he'd just let me reciprocate, if he'd just fucked me like I wanted, I wouldn't have called Sacavè.

"I see, baby," I answered, trying to match Saviour's excitement, trying not to let my guilt show.

I pulled my truck into the garage. Saviour was already unbuckling himself, ready to jump in and drive it right now.

"You can drive it tomorrow after school, okay? Mommy has things to do," I promised, even though he was begging to drive it now, his little hands already on the steering wheel.

It was Sunday, which meant I still had to do meal prep for the upcoming week and fold the laundry that I slept with all over the bed last night.

I brought the flowers inside and stared at them. Pink roses. My favorite color. From a man who was trying to do everything right.

And what did I do? I fucked my ex-husband. The man I'm trying to divorce. The man who's with someone else. The man who represents everything I'm trying to move on from.

I grabbed my phone and looked at it. No missed calls from Tool since yesterday. No texts. Nothing. He'd given me space after I left his house, and I had used that space to make the worst possible decision.

Chapter 8

1 Month Later

Kia, can we talk?

I got a random text from an unsaved number. It had been a month since everything went down. Since I had left Tool's house that night after he'd rejected me. Since I had made the stupid, impulsive decision to call Sacavè at 3 AM. A month of radio silence.

We hadn't spoken since I left his house that night, not a single word. I hadn't even texted or called to say thank you for the flowers or for the mini truck he'd bought Saviour that my son loved so much. Although Sacavè hated it and tried to outdo Tool by buying Saviour a mini version identical to his BMW M6, Savy still didn't favor it as much. He wanted to drive his Chevy every single day, had a fit any time I suggested the BMW instead.

This had been the first time Tool had even reached out, and strangely, it was from a different number. It's not like I had blocked him or anything. He just . . . stopped. He hadn't sent his normal good morning messages that he'd sent every single day since we met. The "good morning beautiful" texts that used to come before I could even brush my teeth. Those just stopped.

I just thought maybe he thought I was too easy after what happened that night. Maybe I had scared him off, or maybe the whole "I'm married" thing finally sank in and he decided I was too much.

I shouldn't even text his ass back. I should leave it on read. But I was curious. I wanted to know why didn't he give me dick that night, and why hasn't he hit me up in weeks? So I texted back.

Should I call? I typed, then hit send before I could overthink it.

He texted back instantly, as if he was waiting on my response. And that felt good. My ego appreciated that he wasn't playing games, wasn't stalling on a reply to prove a point.

Yes, he replied simply.

I didn't let pride get in the way either. I called immediately, ready to hear his voice again after a month of silence.

But when the line connected, I heard a female voice answer.

"Hello?"

I froze. Because I know this nigga was fucking lying. Why would a bitch pick up his phone? So many scenarios ran through my mind in a matter of thirty seconds before I even responded. Was this his ex? His new girl? Some random he'd been fucking for the past month while I was on ice? Was this why he went ghost?

"Who is this?" I asked, my heart racing.

"Kia, it's Sena," she replied.

That's when I realized it wasn't Tool's number after all. It was Sacavè's side bitch bestie, Sena. My only confusion was how the bitch even got my number in the first place. She was intentionally blocked from my old phone, so there wasn't a point in her knowing the new one either.

See, when I cut things off with Sacavè officially, moved out, filed for divorce, I told him I was okay with meeting whatever girl he ended up with. I told him that if she was going to be around my son, I wouldn't mind it. I just needed to have her contact information and have some type of rapport with her. Basic co-parenting respect.

Sena was an exception. She treated my son well, without a doubt. She was an honorable godmother, never missed a birthday, a milestone, anything in Saviour's life. She'd been there since he was born, threw my baby shower, bought him everything. But I absolutely could not find it in my heart to honor her as Sacavè's new girlfriend. I respectfully didn't want shit to do with that side of the spectrum, and I was extremely vocal about it.

So, if she was calling me now, obviously there was some state of emergency. And given that Saviour was in his room sorting ABC blocks, safe and sound, it wasn't about my son. So my next concern was whether my baby daddy was okay.

"Is Sacavè okay?" I asked, because Sacavè was technically still, a month later, my husband. Which makes me next of kin. So in the words of the honorable Kash Doll: *don't nothing move till I sign shit.* I guess whatever happened, I was needed.

"Sacavè is fine. Well, at least for right now," she said, and she was the most soft-spoken and humble I had ever heard her.

"For now? Is he in the hospital or something?" I asked, genuinely concerned at this point. It was evident in my voice because regardless of everything, I still cared for the nigga as my son's father.

"Kia, I called to talk to you because you left some red lace panties at his house, and I wanted to know where y'all stood," she said.

Where we fucking stood.

The audacity. The unmitigated gall. To dissect the side bitch bestie called the wife because she found her panties at a house that had both of their names on the deed and wanted to know where he and his wife stood? I couldn't do shit but laugh at this point. It slipped out.

I must admit that night I slipped and bumped my head and decided to go fuck Sacavè. I wore a red lace set. When I woke up hazily the next morning, trying to get downstairs to cook my son breakfast before he realized what was happening, the only thing on the floor was the red lace bra, my muumuu was still on the stairs where we had left it. I was convinced my panties were somewhere wrapped up in the sheets, but I was too wrapped up in my regrets to look for them properly. Or maybe Sacavè ate them when he ate me from front to back. But again, my focus had been on tending to my son after he caught me and his daddy in bed together.

I had intended on going back upstairs and grabbing them after breakfast, but when Sacavè started to get beside himself with that ring bullshit, and I left completely, forgetting that I even had on panties when I went there in the first place.

I know she called more to get me to confirm or deny whether we were still fucking or not. But after finding my panties there, wrapped up in his sheets, I happen to think there's common sense for that answer. So, I decided to answer the things that she probably didn't know the answers to, things that made more sense to me.

"Well, we're still married because he refuses to sign the divorce papers," I said.

The line got quiet. Like either she didn't know that, or she was told something completely different. Either way, I wasn't here to make shit easy for her. I didn't owe her that.

Before she could even respond, curiosity got me, so I continued. "How did you get my phone number?" I asked.

"I got it from Savy's iPad because I kept asking Cavè for it, but he refused," she answered.

I guess that says he has a little bit of sense, at least. *He didn't mention that to me at all,* I thought. I didn't blame him though, because he absolutely, positively knew better. But then curiosity got me again because although I wasn't going to address the obvious for more reasons than one, I was dying to know one thing.

"How are you sure those are my panties?" I asked, genuinely curious how she had come to that conclusion.

"Well, he said the only two women that spent the night there were me and you, and they're not mine," she answered.

"Did you ask Faith or Marlene?" I asked innocently, referring to his mother and sister. I mean, rightfully, he has a mom and a sister. I was curious if she brought the same audacity to them that she did to "the wife."

"Kia, why would his mother or his sister's draws be wrapped up in his sheets?" she asked.

"And why would his wife's?" I asked back. *Checkmate.*

It sounded a lot like she had the answer to her own questions, but from a female standpoint, maybe she just wanted confirmation. Needed to hear me say it out loud so she could stop lying to herself about what was really going on.

"To confirm: yes, we had sex that night. Yes, those are my panties. And yes, I still want a divorce. Now, are you able to convince him to sign those papers?" I asked, getting to what really mattered to me.

It's safe to say confirmation was exactly what she needed because she hung up immediately after. Didn't say goodbye, didn't cuss me out, nothing. Just *click.*

Now don't get me wrong, I'm a girl's girl. Under different circumstances, I absolutely wouldn't have handled her that way. But I'm not a side bitch consoler, and I damn sure wasn't about to make her feel better about choosing to be with a married man. So there's that.

My next concern was ensuring that Savy wasn't being subjected to any soap opera bullshit at his dad's house.

Whatever drama was going down between Sacavè and Sena, my son better not be in the middle of it.

"Saviourrrr!" I yelled out, calling for him.

I instantly heard his little feet running to me from his room, his iPad in hand.

"Yes, mommy?" he answered, looking up at me.

"Are you okay, son?" I asked, kneeling down to his level.

He nodded, too distracted by his iPad to really process the question. I did my daily check, ran my hands over his arms and legs looking for bruises, checked his face and neck, asked him if anything hurt. It was such a norm for Saviour that he continued to play *Roblox* while I checked him over, not even phased by it. This was our routine after school and after weekend trips to daddy's house.

"Savy, mommy needs to talk to you. Can I borrow your iPad for a second?" I said gently.

When he nodded and handed me the iPad without protest, I got so nervous. Because his answers would make or break a lot of shit, would determine if I needed to go mama bear on Sacavè and Sena both. So I thought for a bit, then started asking carefully.

"Do you like going to daddy's?" I asked.

"Yes," he answered immediately, no hesitation.

"Do you feel safe at daddy's house?" I asked.

"Yes," he answered.

"Is daddy or anyone at daddy's house mean to you?" I asked, my heart pounding.

"No," he answered, shaking his head.

"Do you get whoopings at daddy's house?" I asked.

"No," he answered.

"Who's at daddy's house when you go there on the weekends?" I asked.

He looked at me so confused, as if he wanted to ask what "weekends" even meant. His little face scrunched up, and he just shrugged his little shoulders.

"Who do you see at daddy's house?" I asked, rephrasing.

"TT Sena and daddy and Puff Puff," he answered, counting on his little fingers.

"Who is Puff Puff, baby?" I asked, not recognizing that name.

"TT Sena's doggy!" he answered excitedly, his face lighting up.

"Is TT Sena nice to you?" I asked, the most important question.

"Yes," he answered without hesitation.

"All the time?" I pressed, needing to be absolutely sure.

"Yes, all the time," he answered, nodding his head enthusiastically.

I started to smother him with kisses right then and there because that's all I needed to hear. My baby was safe, happy, and being treated well. That's all that mattered.

I handed him back his iPad and sent him on his way because I had a bone to pick with Sacavè's ass. When I picked my phone back up, I had three missed calls from him. Something about that timing tells me Sena had relayed my message, and he was big mad about it.

"Yes, Sacavè?" I said when I called him back.

"Man, where my son at?" he asked, his voice aggressive and hostile.

"Man, did you try his iPad?" I asked back, matching his energy.

I was trying to figure out where all this hostility was coming from.

"A couple times. It keeps ringing twice then going to voicemail, Kia," he said.

"Okayyy, maybe he keeps pressing decline because he just got his iPad back and he's playing *Roblox*. You cool?" I said, because this wasn't unusual behavior.

This wasn't the first, second, third, or even ninth time Saviour would see me or his daddy calling and decline it to keep playing his game. But Sacavè sounded extra irritated about it now, like something else was going on.

"Nah, I'm not cool. Stop playing with me. I'm 'bout to pull up and see my son," he said. Then he hung up without waiting for my response.

Ten minutes later, he was in my driveway. I just opened the garage from my phone app and yelled out, telling Saviour that his dad was outside.

I heard him taking off running.

"No running!" I yelled out, but he was already gone.

His little feet moved so fast to greet his daddy. I swear, I adored their relationship. It healed the little girl in me to see it, to see a father who showed up, who was present, who loved his son unconditionally even if he couldn't love me right.

I was three minutes behind, walking down to figure out what his problem really was. When I got to the living room, Sacavè was sitting on my couch, smothering Saviour with kisses all over his face while my son giggled and tried to squirm away.

"Nigga, get your shoes off my carpet," I said, pointing at his Jordans tracking dirt on my cream carpet.

He kicked them off where he sat, not even getting up, and Saviour jumped down to go put them neatly at the door like I had taught him.

"What you got going on?" I asked, crossing my arms, waiting for an explanation for this random pop-up.

"Savy, go get your pajamas and stuff out. Daddy will be right there to read you a story and tuck you in," he said to Saviour, ignoring my question.

"I didn't take a bath yet, daddy," Saviour said, looking confused.

"Well, that too," Sacavè said. "Go 'head, I'll be there in a minute."

Saviour ran upstairs, and Sacavè started walking over to me, face scrunched up like he was trying to intimidate me.

"What's under this?" he asked, reaching for the top of my robe, trying to peek inside.

My only thought was that he thought Tool or somebody else was over here, which is why Saviour wasn't answering his calls. But wrong. Now he looks stupid. But I wouldn't be me if I didn't say some smart shit.

"Not red lace panties," I said, smirking.

To be honest, it wasn't shit under my robe but body parts. I only started wearing robes around the house when Savy learned body parts in preschool and started pointing at my yoni, saying "no-no square."

"Ooohhh, that's what this shit about?" he asked, realization dawning on his face.

89

"What shit?" I asked innocently.

"Sena texted my phone talkin' 'bout 'have fun seeing your son after this,'" he said, showing me his phone screen.

Not that anything could, but I hoped she didn't think that weird manipulative shit she pulled was going to make me stop letting Sacavè see Saviour. That's the difference between a bitter baby mama and a wife who knows better. My son's relationship with his father had nothing to do with adult drama.

"She must've texted that before she—" I started to explain.

Before I could finish my sentence, Sacavè was on his knees, face level with my pussy, his finger sliding inside me before I could even react. My pussy was betraying me because why was I so wet? Why was my body responding when my brain was screaming no?

"Nope, we're not doing that. Get up," I said firmly, jumping back and pulling him up by his head.

You only make a mistake once, and I'm not fucking him ever again. Not after last time. Not after the confusion, the regret, the complications.

"She must've texted that before she got on the phone with me," I finished my sentence, smoothing down my robe.

He licked his fingers like he'd just finished eating a five-star meal. Dramatic-ass nigga.

"On the phone? When and how did y'all get on the phone?" he asked, his face a mixture of confusion and anger.

"She said she got my number from Savy's iPad," I said simply, watching his reaction.

I don't know if he was more confused that I was so calm about it, or that she really went as far as getting my phone number out of our four-year-old son's iPad without permission.

"Nah," he said, shaking his head in disbelief.

I guess that's the only word he could muster up right then because he sure was wrecking his brain trying to find more words. In the meantime, I always got something to say.

"When fuckin' your bestie goes wrong, I guess," I said, shrugging.

"Kia, shut up with that," he said.

"Did she tell you I said I still want a divorce?" I asked, getting to the point.

"You told her that?" he asked concerned.

"Did," I confirmed.

He shook his head and rubbed his goatee like he was just so stressed out, like this was all too much for him to process.

"Nah, I ain't spoke to her at all," he said.

"Well, it's thirty minutes past our son's bedtime, so I need you to go ahead and bathe him and tuck him in, please," I said, ready to wrap this conversation up.

That's for him and his side-bitch bestie to figure out. I needed some sleep for work tomorrow. I was working on a promotion that would allow me to be eighty percent remote, and I couldn't afford to be tired and unfocused.

"I'm staying," he stated, not asked.

I couldn't give him pushback on that. I had already told him months ago that he could stay over when he had late pickups or early drop-offs, as long as I was single. Because once I got a man, I knew he wouldn't be going for that arrangement.

"Don't be trying to stay here to avoid your side-bitch bestie," I said as he headed toward the stairs.

He tuned me out, walking up to handle bedtime duties, because he knows I aspire to be the next Desi Banks with my commentary. Always got something to say, always gotta get the last word in.

Chapter 9

My morning was so easy with Sacavè sleeping at the house. I don't miss him specifically. I just miss having a partner. I miss the balance, the teamwork, the way two parents can divide and conquer instead of one person doing everything.

Like last night, when he had Savy in the tub. I could hear them laughing upstairs, Saviour splashing and Sacavè doing his deep voice pretending to be a *Transformer*. Then came the bedtime routine: brushing teeth, reading bedtime stories and tucking him in. While all that was happening, I was downstairs packing our lunches, meal prepping, cleaning the kitchen, doing all the behind-the-scenes work that keeps our lives running.

When I got upstairs, exhausted and ready to crash, Sacavè had run me a bath. Epsom salt, bubbles, my lavender candle lit on the counter. That felt so easy. So natural. So much like the partnership I had always wanted from him but never consistently got when we were actually together.

Of course some weak-ass shit like a bath won't have me running back to no nigga. I'm not confused. I know the difference between appreciating a gesture and wanting the person back. This was just . . . nice. A glimpse of what co-parenting could be like if he wasn't always on bullshit.

Sacavè slept on the floor in Savy's room last night because he couldn't fit in the Lightning McQueen toddler bed with him. If you leave me to assume, he probably would've tried to sleep in my bed but he knew better. He took the floor like a man who understood his place had changed. Or maybe he was just avoiding having to go home and face Sena after that whole panty situation blew up in his face.

Either way, he had to face the music this morning after he dropped Saviour off at school. That was his problem to figure out, not mine.

Tool was on my mind heavy today. Like, consuming my thoughts heavy. I was going back and forth about texting him, replaying that moment at his house over and over, the pleasure, the rejection, the confusion, the month of silence that followed. He had too much restraint for me. The nigga might ignore me and choose self-love or some spiritual shit over dealing with my mess. I don't even know what I would say. What if he changed his number? What if he met someone else? What if he's completely over whatever we were building?

But then I thought about the worst thing he could actually do, and it was ignore me. He wouldn't curse me out, that wasn't his style. He wouldn't be petty; he was too mature for that. The worst-case scenario was silence, and I was already living in that. So what did I have to lose?

I sent a text: "Tool?"

He texted back immediately: "What's up, pretty."

He texted back so fast. I was worried for no reason, working myself up over nothing. But now that I had his attention, I didn't even have a plan. I didn't know what to say, how to bridge this gap, how to address the month of silence. So I went with what I knew best, something safe, something that couldn't be misinterpreted.

"Savy loves his truck," I texted, which was true. My son drove that thing every single day, made vroom-vroom noises, told everyone at school about "my truck like Tool's truck."

"I knew he would. Did you love your flowers?" he texted back.

Of course I did. They were still on my kitchen counter, still fresh somehow, still making me smile every time I walked past them.

"Of course I did," I texted back.

And that was it. He didn't hold a grudge. Didn't give me the cold shoulder. Didn't play games or make me grovel or punish me for the silence. I was used to a nigga throwing fits, giving tit-for-tat energy, making me pay for perceived slights with days or weeks of attitude. Obviously, that's the difference between a nigga and a grown-ass man.

So I did something I had never done before in my life: I asked a man out on a date.

"Lunch?" I texted, my heart pounding like I was sixteen again.

"My pleasure. I'll see you at *Mellow Mushroom* at 12:15. That cool?" he texted back.

Just like that. No "let me check my schedule." No "I'll let you know." No indecisiveness, no making me wait for an answer. Just straight leadership, a plan already formed, a decision already made.

"Yes," I texted back.

It's like everything I prayed for, all in one person.

I was an hour and a half away from lunchtime, and I guess there was nothing else to talk about until then because he didn't reply when I agreed to the location and time. And that was okay. We didn't need to fill every silence with meaningless chatter. The date was set. We'd talk then.

Two hours later, I was thirty minutes late to lunch because a meeting went over. My boss was on one, going over quarterly numbers that could've been an email, and I couldn't pull out my phone to text Tool that I was running behind. I was panicking internally, watching the clock tick past 12:15, then 12:20, then 12:25, imagining him sitting there thinking I stood him up.

Luckily, *Mellow Mushroom* was three minutes from my job. When I pulled up and saw Big Red in the parking lot, I just knew that man didn't give up on me. He waited.

I walked in and saw him sitting at a table facing the door. When I walked over to the table, he stood up like a gentleman. I immediately started to explain.

"I'm so sorry, my meeting ran over and I couldn't—"

He kissed me on my lips, cutting off my explanation mid-sentence.

"Hush, lady. You're worth waiting for," he said.

It's like I want to throw my pussy at this man for any little thing. Must be a hoe. A whole hoe. Better yet, his hoe. I don't know. All I know is that simple statement had me ready to risk it all right there in *Mellow Mushroom*.

All I could manage to say was "Thank you," with this huge sigh of relief, settling in the other side of the booth.

He just stared at me like he was mesmerized, like I was the most beautiful thing he'd ever seen, like the thirty minutes didn't matter at all.

"So what's new? Can I make you mine?" he asked casually.

This man hasn't said shit to me in over a month. Radio silence. Ghost mode. We've been at lunch for five minutes and he's talking about can he make me his? I'm so confused right now. I really want to be toxic as fuck, want to make him explain the silence, want to make him work for it. But he doesn't deserve that shit. He's been nothing but respectful, nothing but intentional, nothing but real.

"Hmm, what's new? Well, I'm working on being promoted to Senior Account Manager, which will make me eighty percent remote. I'm looking forward to that," I said, choosing to share good news instead of diving into the heavy stuff.

"Congratulations," he said, and he said it like he meant it, with this big genuine smile on his face.

But it was like he waited for more. For me to address the elephant in the room. The month of silence. The night at his house. The married thing.

"We need to drink to that one," he said, lifting his lemonade like a toast.

"Absolutely. I find out in two weeks," I said, clinking my glass against his.

"Well, we're gonna celebrate this weekend as a manifestation that it already happened. In Jesus' name," he said with such conviction, such faith.

"Amen," I said, smiling.

He just checked off everything on my build-a-man list. God-fearing, supportive, celebratory, forward-thinking. Other than his disappearing act this past month, I hate that I'm about to really find out what his real problem is. It's like waiting for the red flag to finally reveal itself.

"So can you tell me what happened? From the day I left your house to me texting you this morning, why hasn't there been any formal contact between us?" I asked, deciding to just rip the Band-Aid off.

"Well I mean I called a couple times after you left you never returned my call so I thought maybe you need a time to make a decisions. Have you made them?" he asked.

"Decisions about what, Tevin?" I asked, visibly annoyed now. Shit like this irritated me about Sacavè too, how he always acted like he was unable to express himself clearly. It was almost like I had two sons, like every conversation was a moment to say "use your big boy words."

"First of all, I'm a man. A grown man. And I express myself very well," he said.

Hold up. Did I say that out loud? Why does he always have a way of responding like he can hear my thoughts or something? God, I remember asking you for a nigga that could just read my mind one time. Is this it or something?

"When I say decisions, I'm talking about your marital status. A woman who no longer wants to be married will make sure of it unless they're not sure. Are you?" he said.

"Am I sure?" I repeated, deflecting, doing that little girl shit I hate when other people do it.

Because after he said all that, for my response to be "yes" while I'm still married really doesn't make sense. The thing is, I know I'm done. I moved out almost a year ago. I'm no longer concerned with what he does. We don't communicate unless it's about our son. I'm definitely done with Sacavè as a husband.

"Are you trying to convince yourself?" Tool asked, watching my face.

"Stop doing that," I said, because he was reading my mind again.

"I am sure. But no, I'm not yet divorced," I admitted finally.

"So I can't make you mine?" he said.

And there it was. This man won't let me suck his dick, won't fuck me, disappeared for a month, all for the same reason, because I'm married. But what I'm not understanding is how he made it seem like it wasn't that big of a problem before. He said Sacavè wasn't secure in his position, that he didn't stand on being a husband, that it was clear the marriage was over. But now it's "I can't make you mine" like it's some impossible barrier. What exactly am I expected to do? Force Sacavè's signature on divorce papers?

"Exactly," Tool said.

"Exactly what?" I asked, confused.

This man has got to stop answering my thoughts, or maybe I needed to stop thinking.

"I can't make you mine," he repeated.

He pulled out a wad of money and peeled off two blue faces just as our server was walking over to refill our cups. He slid the two hundred dollars on the table, stood up from his side, took a long sip of his lemonade, and looked at the server.

"Give her whatever else she wants, and then the rest is yours," he said to the server, then looked at me one more time. "Handle your business, Kia."

Then he walked off and left me at the table by my fucking self.

I sat there in shock, watching Big Red pull out of the parking lot to make sure he was serious. And he was. Clearly dead serious. He just left me. In public. At lunch.

"I'll take the rest of my pizza and lemonade to go, please," I said to the server, face full of embarrassment.

I have never in my life had a man leave me in a restaurant. Never. This is so embarrassing. My hands were shaking as I gathered my purse.

When the server came back with my to-go box, she absolutely didn't make it any better.

"Girl, two things," she started, leaning in like we were friends. "If that's your husband, he is fiiine. No offense, you did good. And if he's mad because you had him waiting all that time before you came? You wrong as hell," she said, then snatched up that two hundred dollars so fast and walked off.

Yeah, bitch, because if it was up to me, you wouldn't get no fucking tip. Mind your business.

"I was workinnnng," I called after her, even though I don't know why I bothered defending myself to a stranger.

I left out of there damn near crying. And now I gotta go back to work and sit in my emotions for five more hours. If it wasn't for my promotion, I would leave early.

"That was so embarrassing," I texted him from my truck before pulling out.

"And what is me lusting for a married woman?" he texted back immediately.

Tit for tat. Lesson 142: never hype a nigga up, because as soon as you do, he's going to show you exactly why you should've kept your mouth shut.

But what does me being married even change? I'm not getting married again regardless. I don't want Sacavè. But I also don't want to get toxic or affect my peace trying to divorce him. I've asked for the papers to be signed more times than I can count. More times than I can remember.

Actually, you know what? I'll text Sacavè right now. For shits and giggles. See what excuse he has this time.

When are you signing the divorce papers?

This shit is beating a dead horse at this point. I mean, honestly, we're coming up on a year since I left the nigga. He has a whole girlfriend and everything, and still hasn't signed. He knows it won't affect our co-parenting. He knows I'm done. He just absolutely won't do it.

And now I'm realizing that's exactly Tool's point.

If I really wanted out, I had to make it happen. I had to force the issue. I had to get a lawyer. I had to do whatever it took.

But I haven't.

And that says everything.

Chapter 10

Sena

I'm Sena, Sacavè's best friend of 18 years and counting. We go way back to the sandbox days, to growing up in the same neighborhood where everybody knew everybody. You probably hate me because Kia most likely introduced me as Sacavè's "fake best friend." But respectfully, put some respect on my name.

I'm the one that helped Kia push him to even marry her, so clock that shit. Let's go back.

Every time they had some type of argument, and there were many, Kia was on my phone trying to get me to reason with him. She'd call me crying, venting, asking me to talk sense into him like I was some kind of Sacavè whisperer. It had been after Valentine's Day, about nine years into their on-and-off situation, and she called me complaining about how they'd been together all this time and he hadn't proposed or anything. No ring, no real commitment beyond just existing together.

Now, I'm a daddy's girl. One thing my daddy always told me, even from behind bars during his twelve-year bid, was that a man knows if a woman is marriage material within the first year. If he's not trying to lock you down by then, he's just comfortable. I told Kia that too, tried to give her the game because her dad wasn't in her life to tell her these things. But she didn't want to hear it. She wanted me to make Sacavè want what she wanted.

So I did what she asked. I called Sacavè on three-way and told her to mute her phone. I started off the conversation on some normal shit, asking about his day, talking about some mutual friends, keeping it light. Then I slid it in there, casual as hell.

"When you gonna marry Kia? You know that girl love you down," I said.

"But what does getting married prove?" he said back.

I couldn't agree more that a piece of paper didn't prove shit. A marriage certificate doesn't guarantee loyalty, doesn't stop cheating, doesn't make love last. But I wasn't calling for me.

"A long-term commitment," I said.

He knew it was bullshit too because he hit me with: "Yo ass don't even believe in all that marriage shit like that."

And he was so fucking right. Either I'm with you or I'm not. A wedding doesn't make that more real.

"I'll go to the courthouse right now and marry shorty if that's what she want, but I'm not doing all that extra wedding bullshit and wasting money on one day," he said.

"Man, whatever," I said, not knowing what else to say.

The next day, he went and did that shit. Courthouse wedding, no guests besides me as the witness. Kia got what she wanted, the last name, the legal binding, the title of "wife." They bought a house together two months later. Everything seemed like it was finally falling into place for them.

Then Kia found out she was pregnant.

And then Sacavè got locked up.

Murder charge. For his main man Mally's case that didn't have shit to do with him. Wrong place, wrong time, wrong association. Life started to spiral from there for everybody. Legal beast Careton Matthews had to argue his innocence, build a case from nothing, fight a system that didn't care about the truth. Kia had to start working, providing for herself and the baby growing inside her. And me? I had to console her emotional ass through the whole pregnancy while also being the only constant presence in Sacavè's life while locked up.

She didn't take his arrest well at all. Not that I expected her to, but it was bad. She lost hella weight even though she was supposed to be gaining it for the baby. Every week when we'd go to his visitation at Clayton County Jail, walking up those five flights of stairs because the elevator was always broken, all she did was cry to him about going through her pregnancy all alone.

Mind you, this man was fighting a life sentence or even the death penalty for some shit he didn't even do. Sitting in a box, eating nasty food, sleeping on a thin-ass mattress, watching his life fall apart through phone calls and visits.

I didn't want to say it out loud because it sounded harsh, and Kia was fragile enough as it was. But all I could think was: *he has bigger fish to fry than your pregnancy complaints right now. He's trying not to die in prison.*

At six months, right after the gender reveal party that I had planned and paid for, she stopped going to his visitations every weekend. Said it was because she couldn't handle walking up and down those five flights of stairs every time, that it was too much on her body, that the baby was sitting low and it hurt. Valid concerns, I guess. But it felt like an excuse. Like she was abandoning him when he needed her most.

I hadn't missed a single visitation. Not one. My dad told me that visits were what took inmates outside of the bullshit that was jail. For one hour, two hours, whatever time you got, you weren't an inmate. You were a son, a brother, a friend, a father. You were human again.

So I went every weekend. I was the one that told Sacavè that Saviour was going to be a boy, well before he got the pictures in the mail from Kia weeks later. I was there when his face lit up and he said, "A son. I'm having a son."

He was so proud to have a mini-me. But the pain of possibly being unable to raise him, to teach him how to be a man, to be there for his first steps and first words and first everything that bothered him. I could see it eating him up.

"I can't stomach another nigga raising my son, Nana," he told me during visits. "I can't do it. I'll lose my mind in here if I think about Kia moving on and some other nigga being daddy."

I don't have any kids. I couldn't fully relate to that fear. But I do know my daddy was HIM from prison. His physical absence didn't change our bond, didn't make me love him less, didn't erase him from my life. I didn't know another way. He was locked up for most of my childhood, and I turned out fine.

But Sacavè couldn't see it that way. All he could see was missing everything.

The baby shower that Kia's mother practically forced her to have because let's be real, Kia didn't want to celebrate anything without Sacavè there, but I came around, and I planned the whole thing. Picked the theme, ordered the decorations, coordinated the food, sent the invitations, everything. Kia just showed up.

She hadn't wanted to do maternity photos either because, in her words, it was "embarrassing to be a married single mother." I told her fuck what everybody else thought and go with what she knew.

Four months later, Sacavè was still being denied bond, his case moving at a snail's pace through a system that didn't give a fuck about justice. Then COVID hit and slowed everything down even more. Courts shut down, trials postponed, the whole legal system in chaos.

Kia went into labor alone. No visitors allowed in the hospital due to COVID restrictions. Even if Sacavè had been free, they might not have let him in given how strict the protocols were. So my girl had to push out a whole baby, go through hours of labor, deal with the pain and fear and overwhelming emotion of becoming a mother for the first time, completely alone.

I couldn't be there physically, couldn't hold her hand or wipe her forehead or tell her she was doing good. So I called her on FaceTime two to three times a day, once to see my godson, to check on her, to make sure she wasn't drowning in postpartum depression on top of everything else.

I was there for his first bath at home, for his shots, for his newborn pictures, for when he got circumcised and Kia was beside herself with worry. When she finally got to bring him home and settle into a routine, I damn near moved in. I was changing diapers, holding Saviour while Kia showered or napped or just cried from being tired.

I was the baby daddy at that point.

Clayton County Jail had switched to video visits due to COVID, so that's how Sacavè met his son for the first time. Through a screen. Seeing his boy's face, unable to hold him, unable to smell that newborn smell, unable to be there.

It was the first time I had ever seen my best friend cry. And I mean really cry, not just tears, but that deep, soul-crushing crying. Between me, Kia, and her mom, there wasn't a dry eye in the room witnessing that moment. A father meeting his son through a screen, from a jail cell, for a crime he didn't commit.

My routine became a cycle: classes for my nursing degree, work, and their house. I practically moved into their guest room, sleeping there most nights just to help with Saviour. Months passed like that. Kia was nearing the end of her maternity leave, and thankfully, due to COVID, she was able to work remotely. But she still needed daytime hands-on help with a newborn.

That's when Sacavè offered to pay me to be a live-in nanny. He even suggested I quit my job.

"That's my baby, Nana. I need to know he's good, and you the only one I trust like that," he'd told me during a video visit.

So I did that shit. No questions asked. Quit my job, moved in fully, dedicated myself to raising Saviour while his parents figured out their lives.

Within a couple months of me being full-time help, some wild shit happened. The sheriff who'd been running Clayton County with an iron fist started getting investigated for all the corrupt shit he'd been up to for years. Including letting certain gang members skate on charges, one specifically that connected to Sacavè's case in a way that proved his innocence.

C. R. Matthews Law Firm argued his case with this new evidence, cosigned the lawsuit against the county for wrongful imprisonment, and boom, my best friend was free after 387 days. Over a year of his life gone, a year of his son's life he'd never get back.

Now, don't get me wrong. Kia having resentment for Sacavè not being there for her whole pregnancy and childbirth was warranted, respected, and understood. I never tried to invalidate her feelings about that. But for fuck's sake, it wasn't intentional. It was clearly a misunderstanding, a miscarriage of justice. He didn't choose to be locked up. He didn't abandon her on purpose.

God himself couldn't come down and get that through her thick-ass skull though.

Let my mama and sisters tell it, I didn't know what that felt like so I didn't need to be telling her how to feel. Alright, cool. But that man tried everything when he got home.

He went legit. Got a 9-to-5 blue-collar job at a plant. He made sure that legal mishap couldn't happen again, that he'd never be caught in a situation that could take him away from his family.

When the lawsuit money hit and it was a good grip, six figures for wrongful imprisonment, Sacavè bought Kia a BMW X6, bought himself a BMW M6, and bought me a BMW 328i in appreciation for holding it down. Then he upgraded Kia's courthouse wedding ring to a 2-carat diamond and put the rest in an account for Saviour's future.

I applauded everything Sacavè did. Thought he was being a stand-up nigga, a provider, a father who was making up for lost time in every way he could.

Kia just saw it all as shit he was supposed to do. Like it wasn't enough. Like it would never be enough.

My dad was in the middle on that debate. He said yes, a man is supposed to provide, but that shit is supposed to be appreciated too. He'd known Sacavè since he was knee-high to a grasshopper so he gave his opinions freely.

He also went into this whole spiel one night about how it was obvious that men loved unconditionally and women did not. Because when a nigga wasn't doing for a woman or wasn't there for her, even if it's not his fault, she stopped loving him. But a woman could just bring sex, dinner, and companionship to the table, and a nigga would love her anyway, regardless of what she did or didn't provide.

That TED Talk had me and Sacavè bussin' our heads that night because, honestly, men did love with NO conditions. Or at least, fewer conditions than women.

Months passed. More complaining from Kia. More nagging about what he wasn't doing right, what he needed to change. More ungratefulness for everything he was trying to do.

Then she hit him with wanting a divorce.

I suggested he give it to her. I said verbatim: "Sign that shit for peace, bestie, because goddamn." Sacavè had tried everything under the sun, and that woman was still not pleased. Even worse, he'd only married her in the first place because that's what she wanted, not because he was ready.

He loved her though, so of course he fought it. Begged her to reconsider. They started going to counseling, weekly sessions that worked for them. Kia promised to never ask for a divorce again. I moved back home to give them space to work on their marriage. Saviour was happy. Everything seemed cool for a while.

I was still very present in Saviour's life. His first steps? I was there. First words? I was there. Every birthday, every milestone, every moment that mattered. I was his godmother, and I took that shit seriously.

Then Sacavè mentioned to me that Kia started having suspicions that we were fucking around. Her reasoning? Every time he wasn't at home, his location was at my house. We'd be watching games, hanging out like we'd done since we were kids. Or maybe he was escaping Nagville.

But on everything I love, on my daddy, on Saviour, on God himself, other than some harmless flirting that we'd been on since we were kids, we never looked at each other like that. Never crossed that line. Never even came close.

Kia started acting hella weird toward me though. Stopped inviting me to things, stopped responding to my texts, gave me short answers when we did talk. She told Sacavè it was "woman's intuition."

Woman's intuition, my ass. It was insecurity and projection.

On Saviour's fourth birthday, our friendship really pushed her to the limit, I assume.

Sacavè had paid event planners to throw a Paw Patrol-themed birthday party, bounce house, face painting, the works. I had texted Kia weeks in advance letting her know I was getting custom shirts made for the family and requested her family's sizes. She never texted me back.

Come to find out later, I was blocked. So her childish ass didn't get the memo about the shirts.

Kia pulled up to the party dressed in a Burberry collar shirt, white tennis skirt, and Burberry shoes. Saviour matched her with his little Burberry outfit coordinated to hers. Sacavè had matched them too initially, wearing his Burberry fit.

But then he slipped on his "Father of the Birthday Boy" Paw Patrol shirt over his Burberry drip. And I had on my "Godmommy of the Birthday Boy" shirt.

115

We looked like the parents. We looked coordinated. And Kia's family lost their minds.

She let her family members influence her into thinking I wanted to match him because we were together. That I was trying to play stepmom. That I was disrespecting her at her son's birthday party.

They even asked me to leave. Called me all kinds of shit I didn't respond to out of respect for Sacavè and Saviour. I just left.

Apparently, that same day, she asked Sacavè for a divorce again.

I was so confused about how a nice gesture turned into that.

That night, Sacavè came over to my spot drunk out of his fucking mind. Barely able to stand, slurring, complaining about how his marriage was over, how Kia wouldn't listen to reason, how I was somehow the reason he'd married her in the first place and now the reason she was leaving.

"You told me to marry her, Nana. You said it's what she wanted," he'd said.

We fell asleep on the couch.

Next thing I know, I woke up to his mouth on my pussy.

And before you jump to conclusions and assume all kinds of shit, dragging my name through the mud, that had never happened before that day. Not once in eighteen years of friendship had we ever crossed that line.

But it felt too good to stop him. His tongue was doing things I had never experienced. And I was hurt, and confused, and maybe a little bit in love with him even though I had never admitted it out loud. So I let it happen.

And now we're here.

A couple days ago, Kia asked for my help advocating for a divorce from the man I'm currently sleeping with.

She hates me so much, has made it clear in every way possible but I'm always good enough when she needs something. Good enough to advocate for Sacavè to do what she wants.

I got something for all that energy though.

Chapter 11

My affirmations of a real bitch
You on yo shit
You on yo shit
You da one ain't nobody fucking wit Dafuq
Hype me up, hype me up
Hype me up
I hype me up

The

I usually listened to R&B until I dropped Saviour off at school in the mornings because he was at the stage where he repeated every curse word, every lyric, every phrase he heard. His teacher had already called me once about him saying "what the helly" in class, and I had to explain that yes, mommy needs to watch her mouth. But this morning, I felt too damn good to care.

Vibing to *Flippa T* was my way of saying my affirmations before the day even really started. This was in addition to the ones I had already said with Saviour during our morning regimen.

Today was the day I find out about my promotion, and to be honest, I already knew I had it. I had already claimed it, spoken it into existence, prepared for it like it was done. Over the weekend, I had turned my spare room into my new office space, bought a desk from IKEA, got a cute rolling chair, hung up motivational prints on the wall. I had even prayed over that space, asked God to bless my work, to let this new chapter be everything I needed it to be.

Saviour's birthday was also eighteen days away. This month was going to be full of celebration, full of wins, full of new beginnings. I could feel it in my spirit.

I dropped Saviour off at school, watched him run into the building. Then I continued my drive to work with upbeat and affirming music blasting.

My time management was so good this morning that I even had time to stop at Starbucks to get my triple espresso iced caramel macchiato. I needed to keep my energy upbeat all day, needed that caffeine to carry me through whatever this day had in store.

I walked into work so happy, greeting everyone. You would've thought I had a nigga at home that dug me out all night with the pep in my step.

My workday went all the same as usual until my supervisor, Mike, PM'd me around 2:45 asking me to meet him in his office at 3:00.

It was the moment of truth.

I walked into his office like I was oblivious as to why I was there, playing it cool. But let's be for real, I knew exactly why I was there. This was it. The promotion announcement.

When I got in though, Mike a.k.a. Mr. Rarely-Ever-Serious, the supervisor who usually joked around and kept things light, was a little too serious for me. His face was stern, his posture stiff, his energy completely different from his normal laid-back vibe.

If nothing had humbled me up until that point, his stiff-ass attitude did it. My confidence deflated fast. All I could think about was how I had already set up my home office, already started planning how I'd use the extra money. What if I didn't get it? What if someone else did? What if I had been too confident, too presumptuous?

Then he hit me with: "So I have a few things to discuss with you, Kia."

My anxiety shot through the roof. All I could do was nod. A few things? What few things? Just tell me if I got the promotion or not!

Then the desk phone rang, and he answered it. "Mike speaking . . . yeah . . . uh-huh—okay."

I was literally sitting in my seat about to have a full panic attack at this point. My leg was bouncing uncontrollably. My mind was racing through every possible scenario. Did I mess something up? Did someone complain about me? Did they choose someone else and now Mike had to break the news gently?

He was about two minutes into his conversation, talking about some client issue, when I mouthed across the desk: "Would you like for me to excuse myself?"

He covered the receiver with his hand and said, "I'm sorry, yes please. And do you mind grabbing me a water from the break room?"

I nodded and mouthed "sure." In my head I was spiraling: *So I got demoted to assistant or some shit? Why is he making me get him water? This is humiliating.*

I walked down the hallway toward the break room, my mind preparing for the worst. I pushed open the door and—

"SURPRISE!"

The entire break room yelled out. Confetti cannons went off. My whole team was there: Myra, Eric, Jamila, Trey, even people from other departments I barely talked to. The break room had "CONGRATULATIONS" balloons and streamers everywhere, a cake that said "Congrats, Kia!" in purple frosting.

Mike walked right in behind me, that serious face breaking into the biggest smile.

"Congratulations on your promotion, Kia," he said, shaking my hand firmly, then pulling me into a hug.

This was the Mike I knew, the joker, the one who couldn't resist a good setup. He definitely played me real good just then. Had me thinking I was about to get fired when really I was getting promoted.

But yes, your girl got the promotion! Senior Account Manager, eighty percent remote, significant pay increase, better benefits, more flexibility. Everything I had been working toward for the past two years.

My work besties were so happy for me. Myra was crying actual tears, hugging me so tight. Eric was hyping me up, saying he knew I had got it. Jamila was already talking about celebrating after work.

"We're going out for drinks," Myra said. "Twin Peaks, right after work. I'm not taking no for an answer."

I didn't have a problem with a couple espresso martinis to celebrate. I had earned this. We'd earned this, me and my little team who'd supported me through everything.

The workday carried on mostly the same after that, except now I was packing up some of my stuff, my desk decorations, my favorite pens, my framed picture of Saviour, things I needed to take home to set up my remote workspace. It was bittersweet. I would miss seeing Myra and Eric every day, miss our lunch breaks and office gossip sessions. Now we'd have different schedules, different off days. I'd be home most of the week.

But on the upside? I'd be able to cook homemade meals for my son instead of always packing cold lunches. I'd be able to pick him up from school from time to time instead of that always being his dad's responsibility. I'd have more flexibility, more freedom, more time with Saviour.

Another adjustment would be the rotating weekends. I'd have to work some Saturdays now. But with the pay increase and everything else? Chile, I'll make it work.

The workday came to an end, and no lie, it seemed to have gone by faster than any other day. Maybe it was the excitement.

I walked out of the building with a box full of things, my desk plant, my "Black Girl Magic" mug, and files. As I approached my truck in the parking lot, I noticed a "CONGRATS!" balloon clamped to a manila envelope and stuck between my windshield wipers.

I didn't know what it was or who it was from, but celebrating me was always appreciated. Any acknowledgment of my hard work, my growth and success.

I tapped my key fob to pop the trunk, set the box in there, and closed it. Then I walked around to the driver's side and removed the envelope from the window, the balloon bobbing in the cold Georgia wind. I slid into my seat with a smile, tossing the envelope and balloon on the passenger seat.

First things first, I needed to get my car started and turn my seat warmers on because Georgia weather was more bipolar than I was. It was 72 degrees yesterday, and today it was 43. Make it make sense.

As soon as I went to reach for the envelope to see what was inside, I heard knocking on my window. Aggressive knocking.

"Girl, I'm riding with you!" Myra yelled through the glass, already pulling on the door handle. "DP can come get me from Twin Peaks later. I'm not standing out here in this cold-ass weather."

I didn't have room to say no even if I wanted to, she was already yanking on the handle, doing a cold dance. I swear Myra was one of the most boujetto bitches I had ever come across in my life. She had dimple piercings, a tongue piercing, and long 25mm lashes. Her work voice was completely different from her outside voice. At work, she was professional and polished, but outside? She was West Side Atlanta to the bone, baby. Ratchet as hell, loud as hell, and I loved her for it.

I popped the locks so she could hop in. She snatched the envelope and balloon from the passenger seat before I could grab them.

"Nuh-uh, bitch, I do not want my ass hot," she said, immediately tapping at the control panel, trying to figure out how to turn off the seat warmer. "How you turn this shit off?"

I couldn't do shit but laugh. It was always kicks and giggles with my girl. "It's the button with the seat and the wavy lines, Myra."

"Girl, this car got too many buttons. You boujee as hell," she said, finally finding it and clicking it off.

"What's that?" she asked, pointing at the envelope that was now in my lap.

"Girl, hell if I know," I said, then tossed it in the backseat. I wanted to open it alone, to be honest. No offense to Myra, but this felt personal, and I didn't want to share that moment with anyone else.

I had a short list in my mind of who it could be from. It could've been my little work boo Trey. It could've been

Tool, maybe he sent something sweet. I mean, everybody knew I was finding out today, so there was no telling.

I pulled out of the parking space while Myra scrolled through her phone, then started messing with my car's touch screen.

"Girl, how do I play music? This truck too boujee for me," she said, pressing random buttons, pulling up the navigation, the climate control, everything except the music.

We both busted out laughing. I showed her in one tap.

"Girl, it's right there," I said, pressing the music icon.

As soon as I tapped it, Flippa T started blasting from where I had had it on repeat all morning.

—I hype me up, I hype me up . . .

We were turned up all the way to Twin Peaks. But even with all that energy, I couldn't get my mind off what the fuck was in that envelope. My eyes kept looking to the backseat in the rearview mirror. What if it was something important? What if it was something bad?

An all-expenses-paid vacation would be nice, I thought.

***

When we pulled up to Twin Peaks, the parking lot was already half full with the happy hour crowd. Myra and I walked in, found seats at the bar, and immediately got the attention of the bartender, a fine-ass light-skinned nigga with a fade and a smile that could sell anything.

"Yes, I'll take an espresso martini, please," I said, not even looking at the menu. That had been my drink order everywhere I went now. My hairstylist had put me on to them months ago, and I hadn't turned back since.

"Girl, you are too boujee," Myra said, shaking her head. "I just want a Don Julio Reposado lemon drop with extra sugar rim."

If I got a dollar every time Myra called me boujee, I'd be a millionaire by now. I swear she clocked everything I did as boujee: my drink order, my car, my purse, my shoes, the way I pronounced certain words. But Don Julio Reposado wasn't exactly house liquor either, and that's exactly why I called her boujetto.

As soon as we got our drinks, the others started coming in. Eric walked in with his loud laugh, dapping up the bartender like they were old friends. Jamila came in on the phone, probably with her man, telling him she'd be home later. Trey walked in looking fine as hell in his work slacks and a fitted button-down, sleeves rolled up showing his forearms. And surprisingly, even Mike showed up, loosening his tie as he sat down.

"Let's get a round of shots for everybody on my tab," Mike announced, pulling out his credit card and sliding it to the bartender.

"Aw shit, Mike, don't start no shit!" Trey said, grinning.

Mike was never one of those uptight-type bosses. He was chill 98% of the time, cracking jokes, bringing donuts, asking about our personal lives, treating us like humans instead of just employees. The other 2% of the time was when job performances weren't being met or someone was slacking. Then he'd turn into a different person: sharp, direct, not playing any games. I rarely had to see that side of him because I stayed on top of my work. But I had seen him read people for filth when they deserved it, and the way he'd go in? It would confirm that he was for sure one of the gworls. Had the sass, had the reads, had the neck rolls and everything.

We all told the fine-ass bartender what kind of shot we wanted. I went with Casamigos, Myra got Don, Eric wanted Hennessy, Jamila requested vodka and Trey got Gin.

Mike stood up and raised his shot glass. "If the river was liquor, and I was a duck I'd drink my way down and swim my way up, but the river isn't liquor and i'm no duck so let's take these shots and get fucked up!"

We all tapped our glasses together, then tapped them on the counter and threw them back. I chased it with my espresso martini, which wasn't even halfway done yet.

"Next round on me, 'cause my girl got promoted!" Myra yelled out.

The bartender was fixing another drink but still turned around and said, "Coming right up, beautiful."

I just shook my head. I took my first shot on an empty stomach and now shot number two was on the way. Don't get me wrong, I used to be a fish back in the day. Liquor was my specialty before I had my son, back when I had dick at the house and didn't have to worry about waking up at 6 AM to pack lunches and do school drop-off. But now, with my son and no dick at the house, I was a little boring. It was either one espresso martini at the bar with coworkers or me and my girl Miss Taylor at the house on the couch.

For some reason, I always correlated liquor with sex. Maybe it was because every wild night I'd had in my twenties ended with me in someone's bed. Maybe it was muscle memory. But unless I was willing to double back on Trey or call Sacavè, I needed to slow down.

Trey's dick was good as fuck, probably the best I had ever had, if I'm being completely honest. But fucking my coworker was a setup for destruction. Everybody else at work thought we just flirted a lot, that I called him my "work boo" as a joke. Myra was the only one outside of us who knew we'd actually fucked. And she only found out because Trey started being super territorial after we slept together, giving other niggas dirty looks when they talked to me, sitting next to me at every meeting, texting me outside of work. Myra don't miss a beat, so she pulled me aside one day and asked: "Y'all fucking?"

And I told her everything. When I told Trey he was acting pussy-whipped, that he needed to fall back before people caught on, he pulled away so hard we barely even spoke anymore. I was surprised he even came to Twin Peaks today with his emotional-ass.

Anyway, the next round of shots came. Mike did his little chant and we threw shot number two back.

The drinking continued. Conversation flowed. We ordered wings, loaded fries, fried pickles, all the bar food that would soak up the alcohol and give us a fighting chance at not being completely gone.

Myra tapped out first because her man, DP, texted saying he was outside. I really think she hit her limit and texted him for a rescue. Then Mike tapped next, saying he had an early meeting and needed to be functional tomorrow.

By then, I was two espresso martinis and four shots deep, feeling good. So I went ahead and texted Sacavè: "Celebrating my promotion. Can you keep Saviour overnight? I'll pick him up from school tomorrow."

Me, Trey, Eric, and Jamila were still drinking, still laughing, still celebrating.

Trey had scooted down so he ended up next to me, our thighs touching, his arm casually draped on the seat behind me. He started talking shit about me babysitting my "little weak-ass drink". That was the most the nigga had said to me in months, and now I was stuck proving to him that I could keep up. Pride took over. So now I was five shots in and feeling sexy.

Jamila tapped next, saying she had to get home to her kids. Eric tapped right after, talking about he wasn't about to be a third wheel while me and Trey were "all boo'd up."

I really didn't trust myself with Trey alone, especially not drunk, 'cause that nigga was so fucking fine. 5'9, athletic build, smile that could talk you out of your panties, voice that made your pussy jump. He was the first piece of dick I had had after officially being done with Sacavè. And I swear after that drought, I felt like a virgin again when he finally got inside me. His dick was big, almost too big for me, stretching me in ways I wasn't prepared for but loved every second of.

"Another round," Trey said, and I thought he was asking me, but he was looking at the bartender when I looked up from biting into my wing.

"Trey, no. I am fucked up," I said, and it came out in my sexy, soft tone, the tone that told me I was too drunk and it was time to go. The tone that got me in trouble. I was tapping out. I still had work tomorrow, well, technically I was starting my remote position tomorrow and had to be online by 11 AM. I needed to go home, update my software, test my internet connection, make sure everything was ready.

"One more, Ki. My loft is right there. You don't have to drive too far," he insisted. "Last one. On me," he said.

"Okay, last one," I agreed, and we toasted. He said something about elevation and new heights, we tapped the counter in unison, and took the shots.

The fact that Trey mentioned his loft told me he just knew he was getting some pussy tonight. Had it all planned out.

"Hey! Can we get our checks, please?" I called out to the bartender, making it clear I meant business.

"One check is cool," Trey said to the bartender, then winked at me. "The celebration is on me."

Honestly, knowing that I had to see Trey way less now because of my promotion made the thought of doubling back not seem too bad. I would probably only see him on one of my in-office days, if that. Seeing him wasn't the issue as much as making it obvious that we had something going on. Everyone knew I was technically married, and not many people knew I was actively trying to divorce Sacavè, so it looked weird.

Anyway, he paid the tab, over $200 for our drinks and food, and I handled the tip, sliding two twenties across the bar.

As we were walking out into the cold night air, all I could think about was how thankful I was for the self-drive feature on my car. Trey's loft was only a half mile away. He offered for me to just ride with him and come back to get my truck in the morning, but with my work equipment and personal items in there, I refused.

Before I pulled off, I checked my phone to see if Sacavè had texted back.

"Bet. Congrats. Sena gonna have to drop him 'cause I got OT tomorrow. Gotta be there at 6 AM."

As soon as I read that text, I wished I had seen it sooner. Because then I would've stopped drinking, would've made it back home in time for Sacavè to drop Saviour off, and I could've taken him to school myself.

Sena was intentionally NOT on the pickup list at Saviour's school because I didn't want her to have the luxury of picking up my baby whenever she felt like it. But the school didn't care as much about who dropped him off in the mornings, they just cared about who could take him. Sacavè could've lied. Saviour would've told me eventually, but still.

"I guess if that's the only option. Thanks," I texted back.

But there was nothing I could do about it now. I was drunk, celebrating, and about to make a decision I'd probably regret in the morning.

Chapter 12

Those thirteen minutes to Trey's loft felt like forever in Atlanta traffic, even though the man literally lived half a mile from the bar. I don't know how he got there before me, but he did. He was already parked and upstairs by the time I pulled into the garage. He buzzed me in, and as soon as I parked, I switched out of my heels into the Crocs I kept in my truck, then hopped out and took the elevator up.

I felt like I was floating, that's how drunk I was.

As soon as Trey opened the door to his loft, I walked straight past him to his couch and laid out flat. I didn't remember which direction his bedroom was in, or if I could even make it there if I tried. My head was spinning, and all I wanted was to be horizontal.

"Here, drink some water," he said, handing me a bottle of Fiji water.

"Open it," I said, handing it back to him without even trying. I didn't have the strength to do shit but lay down.

He cracked the top and handed it back to me, then sat down at the other end of the couch. He took my Crocs off and started rubbing my feet. Not only did he have a foot fetish, his foot massages felt like sex, and he loved sucking toes too.

"Let's go to the bed," he said after a few minutes, still rubbing my feet, working his thumbs into my arches.

"You gotta carry me," I said. If he wanted me to go anywhere else in this loft, he'd have to physically transport me there.

And he did. He threw me over his shoulder like I weighed nothing and smacked my ass as he carried me toward his bedroom.

"Wait, put me down real quick," I said before he could toss me on the bed.

That liquor was running through me. I had to pee, plus I wanted to get out of my work clothes. My biggest pet peeve was outside clothes on the bed. His floor-to-ceiling windows always made me feel exposed, like somebody in another building could see us, but honestly, in that moment, I didn't even care. The whole city could watch.

When I came out of the bathroom, Trey was laid back on his bed watching me. I walked over to his windows to look at the view. The Atlanta skyline at sunset was beautiful. It was always a dream of mine to live in a high-rise like this, but with Saviour being so wild and energetic, the thought of him near these floor-to-ceiling windows terrified me.

"That shit don't make no sense," he said. He was less than a foot behind me as I stood there in my bra and thong, admiring the view.

He was admiring me. As soon as I turned around, he was sitting on the side of the bed with his pole long and at attention. I swear that shit had to be like 10 to 11 inches long. My reaction was like the very first time, his dick was his third leg. The contrast never stopped surprising me.

"Come sit on it," he demanded.

I nodded to the side table for him to grab a condom because he always had raw dog desires. Although the condom didn't even go all the way down and he always complained about it being too tight, he still had to wear it. No exceptions.

He grabbed the Magnum XL from the side table, used his teeth and one hand to open it while watching me and using his other hand to stroke it. I watched him as I climbed out of my thong.

All I could think about was how I barely stayed on top when I tried to ride him before. I was never this drunk, though, maybe the liquid courage might change some shit.

"Lay back," I said as soon as he was done rolling it on.

I walked over to him and climbed on top, easing slowly down on it as he held my waist. The stretch was intense, almost too much, but in that good way that made my toes curl.

"Shiiit," was all I could say. I continued easing down, letting out casual moans, trying to adjust to his size.

I tried to focus as his hands moved from my waist to the back of my bra, unhooking it with one hand, releasing my titties. He hated when I kept any clothes on during sex. Said he wanted to see all of me, wanted access to everything.

I was extremely insecure about my stomach and my boobs after my son. I didn't know if he would enjoy me like my baby daddy did. My boobs weren't perky anymore, and my once flat, clear stomach was now flat but tiger-striped. Stretch marks that told the story of growing Saviour, of my body changing to make room for life.

But he still kissed all over it, made me feel like every part of me was perfect.

I was taking my time easing down on it when I guess he got impatient. He sat up, picked me up while still inside me, stood up, sliding deeper, and started to stroke.

"Man, take all that shit," he said as he rammed every inch of his dick inside of me while I was in the air, my legs wrapped around his waist.

"Hold o-o-onnn," I moaned, but he wasn't trying to hear that.

He didn't give a fuck. He knew I liked BDSM and fast penetration, so he gave me that. Gave me exactly what my body was craving even if my mind knew better.

"You missed this dick?" he asked, breathing heavy as he stroked.

I couldn't even form words. I was convinced his tip was tapping on my heart with how deep he was going.

"Did you?" he asked again, his hand moving to hold the back of my neck, forcing me to look at him.

I nodded, unable to speak, unable to do anything but feel.

"Say it," he demanded, his strokes getting deeper.

I tried to say the words, but the shit just couldn't come out. This was the best type of pain I've ever felt, that edge between too much and not enough.

He squatted and put both of my legs on his shoulders, then pinned me to the wall, using it for leverage.

"I love how you taking that shit," he said, looking me in my eyes. "I finally got you in a position where you can't run," he said.

That he did, and I can't say I didn't enjoy this shit. He could feel how much I was into it, my juices were dripping down his pole, then his balls, down his legs too.

Then he pulled out, lifted me above his shoulders and ate me, butterflied against the wall. My hands went to his head, gripping, remembering to only rub his head forward so I didn't mess up his waves.

Finally, I could moan freely. Then he started to tongue fuck me, that was another one of my favorites, the way he worked his tongue.

Then he turned me around, laid me on my back on the bed, and took my pretty pink toes in his mouth while he slid inside of me. It was his favorite position when it was time for him to cum, but my least favorite because his big Mac truck was too big for my garage in this angle. The depth was almost unbearable.

So I grabbed his hand to place it over my mouth to muffle my moans while he did his damage.

"O-o-o-hhh," I moaned through his hand.

Until he busted all in the condom and quickly pulled out to make sure it didn't roll down or pop.

"Shitttt," he yelled out, his body tensing, then relaxing.

"You trouble. Ima miss seeing that lil booty prancing around the office too," he said, catching his breath.

He started to walk to the bathroom, and I jumped up and did the same. I grabbed a rag and towel from the linen closet and turned on the shower.

"Are you?" I said.

"I am," he said, and there was something sad in his voice. Like maybe he was realizing this was probably the last time.

As I showered, something caught my eye, a pink loofahh hanging from the showerhead.

I was immediately disgusted. Not necessarily with him, I mean, we weren't together, but with myself. Because this confirmed what I already knew: I was just another body to him. And given that he never wanted to use protection, that pink loofahh probably belonged to someone who thought she was the only one.

I finished my shower quickly, wrapped myself in a towel, and walked back into the bedroom. Trey wasn't there. I assumed he'd gone to the kitchen or something. I bent over to grab my dress from where I had dropped it, ready to get dressed and get the hell out of there.

But before I could, he was behind me again, making his intentions clear.

I quickly stood up and turned around. "Trey, I gotta go," I said, and my tone was serious enough that he actually backed up.

"Damn, what's up?" he asked, looking confused.

I looked at him, equally confused by his confusion. "I mean, what's up? Thanks for the drinks, appetizers, and the dick too. Gotta go though."

I didn't mean for it to come out as harsh as it did, but that pink loofahh had thrown me completely off. It was a reality check I didn't know I needed.

I grabbed my bra and thong, making absolutely sure not to forget any part of my set this time. I walked into the living room, slid on my Crocs, grabbed my purse, keys, and water bottle, and headed for the door.

He walked me there, looking like he wanted to say something but couldn't find the words.

I kissed him on the cheek. "Thanks, Trey," I said, and then I was in the wind.

Had I not seen that loofahh, I probably would've stayed the night, gotten another round or two, and left first thing in the morning. But I did see it, and now I had to take this twenty-five-minute ride home regretting sex once again.

When I slid back in my car, I peeped the congratulations balloon still floating in the backseat. I had been too hype about my promotion, then too caught up with Trey to even check what it was.

I reached back and grabbed it. My buzz was wearing off now, and I was curious. I ripped the envelope open and pulled out the papers.

My stomach dropped.

Divorce papers.

The same ones I had been on his ass about signing for damn near a year. And there his signature was, big as day across the bottom.

This nigga really signed them.

On my promotion day. Left them on my shit at my job. With a whole congratulations balloon like he was being funny or some shit.

This is what I wanted, right? What I'd been begging for. So why the fuck did my chest feel tight? Why couldn't I breathe?

I needed to talk to him. Needed to hear his voice. I grabbed my phone and called him.

Chapter 13

Sacavè

At this point, I'm probably the villain in the story. And I'm not even here trying to convince you otherwise. I know what kind of nigga I am. I know what kinda shit I been through.

I love Kia with everything in me. And even more than that, I love my son, Saviour. That lil nigga truly changed my life for the better. I may not verbally express all that shit because being vulnerable ain't easy for a nigga, but my actions say it all. I feel like she's just tired of me. I put her through a lot, some of it I didn't even mean to put her through.

I hate that I missed out on her carrying him in her stomach. I hate that I wasn't there when he was born. I hate that I missed his first year of life sitting in a cage for some shit I didn't even do. I hate that I didn't propose to her proper or give her a big-ass wedding because I know women care about little shit like that, feel me?

I did my part though. She never wanted for shit. Any nigga can give her shit, and I promise you on God I gave it all to her before. If I'm being honest, I don't want to sign the papers because I feel like I can still be the nigga she needs. Maybe she can see that there ain't no nigga out there really better than me.

I'm not perfect. Far from it. No nigga walking this planet is. But I'm damn near close.

Maybe I need to start seeing that lady again, the one who wanted to talk about all kinds of trauma and shit. She lowkey fixed some shit before. Or maybe . . . I should get Kia pregnant again and do the shit the right way. Do it how it's supposed to be done. I could be there for every appointment, every ultrasound, the pictures, the baby shower, the gender reveal, the birth. I could get my baby girl and name her Summer like I always wanted. That's when everything changed for us. Having Saviour.

Nothing happened between me and Sena until Kia left me.

Honestly, Sena is not even my girlfriend. She's my best friend, someone other than my wife who knows me better than I know myself. They were really cool until they weren't. One random day it was like Kia flipped a switch. "You fucking her? Fuck that bitch." Just like that.

My wife is my family. It's family over everything. So, if one day Kia told me to choose, the choice was obvious. Sena was out.

Sena is a good-ass godmother though. Kia even said that she loves our son like me and her do. Sena didn't really have no problem with Kia either, not until the other day when she pulled up on me and found Kia's panties in my bed.

The night Kia wanted some but Sena was over at the house. So I told Sena we had to leave, that Saviour had a temperature, and I was taking him to the hospital to get it checked. She knew that meant Kia would be coming to the hospital too. Even if it didn't make sense to Sena, she knew not to push back on anything involving my son. So she left. And I changed my sheets just in time as Kia pulled up. I kicked my best friend out so I could fuck my wife.

That shit was not unheard of.

When I say Kia came through that night looking right . . . she had on a matching lace bra and panty set in my favorite color. That shit had me weak. Then she pulled my dick out and put her warm-ass mouth on it. Her mouth was warmer than a sauna and wetter than Niagara Falls, man. She sucked the skin off my dick like only Kia knew how. *Supa Head* had nothing on her and that's on everything I love.

I moaned from the head she was giving me. Had to stop her at one point because if she kept going like that, I was gonna nut too soon, and a couple rounds would've turned into a half round.

I told her to lay back and started peeling that set off her. When I got to the panties, man, listen, I almost ate them bitches off her. They were so wet. Not just heat wet, dripping wet. Her pussy was freshly waxed too. I ate everything. Went from pussy to ass. Ran my tongue up her ass crack. After about two or three rounds of beating that shit in, her head in the pillow so she didn't wake Saviour up, then we knocked out.

About four hours later, Saviour came running in my room for breakfast like he always does. That shit felt good to me, him waking up to his mommy and daddy in bed together. But I could tell by her reaction it bothered her. She turned red. She was uncomfortable being naked under the sheets in front of our son, even though she always talked about wanting him to see us love on each other.

We went downstairs to handle breakfast. We took out eggs and grits. Then when she came downstairs in that muumuu, ass twisted just right, she went in the freezer and pulled out some shrimp. Made shrimp and grits with scrambled eggs while Saviour played on his iPad and I looked through bills.

I can't lie, I missed that shit. Missed her doing it.

But when I told her that, it made her uncomfortable too.

Sena cooks too, but none of that felt like home. When Kia does it, it's home. When we finished eating and Kia and Saviour left, the house was quiet and lonely again. Then Sena popped back up. She was pissed because she'd been blowing up my phone trying to check on Saviour, but my phone was upstairs.

"Saviour is good, man. Calm down," is all I said before I took off upstairs with Sena on my ass. I started straightening up his room and ignoring her.

I don't know exactly what happened, but she got Kia's number out of my son's iPad and called her. She'd asked me for Kia's number a couple times, but I told her I could tell Kia whatever she needed me to. She thought that was bullshit and did what she wanted.

All I know is whatever Kia said to her had Sena texting my phone with some weird shit. But it didn't seem to bother Kia as much as it bothered Sena. Sena said she felt "tried as a woman",whatever that meant. She knew we were still legally married. She knew I still love Kia. So I knew it didn't have nothing to do with that.

I started to be done with Sena when she texted my phone some shit that sounded like a threat. Like she was either gonna harm my son or find a way to keep him from me. I'm not going for neither one of those. Not now, not ever.

I had to check that shit and still remember I was talking to my best friend. I swear that was hard.

She told me Kia said something like, "I'll pack me and Saviour up and neither one of y'all will see him again." That's why Sena said she went off.

Kia's mouth get lethal, but I don't think Kia said that. And if she did, she would've repeated it too. My baby mama can fight like on some Laila Ali type shit learned that the first and last time I played in her face. She fucked this one bitch up had her leaking she had to go to Grady. Kia don't play those games with my son though, and she knows not to. I had to make sure Sena understood that too.

The shit blew over for a little bit. Then a couple weeks later, me and Sena were in the car when Kia texted me about wanting a divorce. The CarPlay read it out loud, unsolicited, like we hadn't said two words to each other all day.

Sena got so mad all over again for no reason and flipped her shit, putting her hands on me and calling Kia all types of bitches. I had to pull over because Cobb County don't fuck around, and she had me swerving.

I pulled into the Kroger parking lot trying to reason with her. As soon as I said, "Stop calling Kia out of her name," she got out the car and started walking.

Allah be my witness, I don't do scenes in public. I don't do embarrassment, especially not in Cobb County. I know there's no winning with the police, so I left her ass there. Only she knows why she decided to get out, because I didn't put her out. I wouldn't have either. I wish a nigga would put my mama or sister out of a car somewhere.

I called Kia to tell her what just happened and to address the text she sent.

She sounded like she was crying. But she's one tough-ass motherfucka. Nothing too tough to make her cry. She didn't want to talk about it, so I figured either she was on her period or some nigga did something to her.

She'd sent that text 30 minutes ago though, so of course, I asked, "Are you crying because you want a divorce, Kia?"

She said, "Nigga, please. I cried my cry about you enough."

That's when I told her about how her text had Sena losing her shit. The story had her laughing instead of crying, and that's all that mattered to me. Kia deserved to always be happy, man. She's an amazing person.

She told me she had to get back to work. I told her I wasn't signing the papers and that was that.

She had some Hulk nigga around my son the other day too. I wasn't feeling that at all. If I didn't pull up to bring my son food, I wouldn't have even known another nigga was at the house around my son.

I'm an active father. That stepdad shit is super dead. Ain't nobody playing house with my wife and my son but me.

He brought my son a truck like his. If my son didn't like it so much, it would be in the next trash pickup. That shit hurt me though. I can't imagine another man playing the role Sena plays in my son's life because Saviour adores her. And when I think about it, maybe that's what really bothers Kia about Sena. But she's been around for so long, through so much shit, that it shouldn't even matter anymore.

I wish I could go back and not cross that line with Sena. Even now, we don't fuck often because it truly wasn't supposed to happen. Sex between us has no excitement. I just feel like I'm fucking my friend. It's hard to explain.

Kissing her feels strange. Like I don't feel shit.

I don't even have real feelings for her. I just love my best friend. I love how she loves my son. I love how she loves me. But I'm not in love with her.

I'm an honest nigga 90% of the time, so believe me when I say she knows how I feel. She talks to me about other niggas to this day, and I give her advice. But also as a man, if she pulls up trying to wrap them big-ass lips around my dick, I don't stop her.

With Kia it's the complete opposite. I feel territorial over her. She's my wife. Like a kid's favorite toy, that's my ball. That pussy is top two. The head? Valedictorian. The kisses never feel wrong. I enjoy being in her guts. I love her so much. She gave me my son, for that I'm thankful beyond words.

I can't let that go.

Signing those divorce papers would make me feel like I failed Allah and, most of all, I'd be failing my son. He deserves a two-parent home with his mommy and daddy together.

And I'm not giving up on making that happen.

Chapter 14

"Sena, where Sacavè at?" I asked, calm, even though my heart was pounding.

The fact that this bitch saw my picture pop up on his screen and still answered tells me she likes biting off more than she can chew. She wanted some type of confrontation.

"He sleep right here," she said, sounding satisfied. Like she won something.

She was definitely trying to be cute. Trying to make me feel some type of way. But I'd be a dumbass to let her see me sweat, so I kept my cool as much as I could. Reminded myself that I don't even want him anymore; it's just the principle. You know I don't care for you, so why answer his phone? Why insert yourself into a conversation that has nothing to do with you?

"And my son?" I asked.

"He's asleep in his room," she answered, and I could hear the facetious tone. Like she'd put him to bed. Like she was playing house with my family.

"Okay, thanks, boo. Can you tell Sacavè to call me when he wakes up?" I asked, killing her with kindness even though I wanted to reach through the phone.

"Definitely," she said, matching my nice nasty tone.

"Th—" Before I could even finish saying thank you, she hung up the phone.

Click.

And that told me all I needed to know. She wanted to feel powerful. Wanted to prove something.

I sat there in my car in Trey's parking garage, staring at my phone screen.

I'm not hurt or mad about him finally signing the divorce papers. That's what I wanted. What I had been asking for. What I had been begging for, really, for almost a year.

It's about how he did it. The classless act of doing it on the day of my promotion, a day that should've been about celebrating me, my accomplishments, my growth, and sticking it on my fucking car window at my damn job with a congratulations balloon attached.

But the papers are signed. His signature is on there. And I'll definitely get them in my attorney's hands first thing Monday morning before he even thinks about changing his mind.

Right now, I just needed to get home, sober up, and get some sleep. Process everything.

***

My usual 6:30 AM alarm went off, pulling me from a restless sleep full of dreams I couldn't quite remember but left me feeling unsettled. I usually woke up this early to give myself time to get me and Saviour ready, making breakfast, brushing teeth, locating the other shoe that always went missing. But with him being at Sacavè's with Sena, it gave me a lot more time. Too much time, actually. Time to think.

That part irritated me. But not as much as the fact that Sacavè hadn't even returned my call from last night. Hadn't texted. Hadn't reached out.

I got rest, yes. My body needed it after all that liquor. But I woke up with a heavy heart, with this weight sitting on my chest that I couldn't shake. For almost a year, I had been asking him for a divorce, begging him to sign those papers, threatening him with lawyers and court dates. And he finally did it.

But now I was in a state of shock. Anxious. Like, what's next? What does life look like on the other side of this? Who am I without being Sacavè's wife? I had been somebody's wife for 4 years, but I had been trying to be his wife for almost ten years before that.

And now it was over.

I started my morning regimen on autopilot, washing my face first with my charcoal cleanser, then brushing my teeth with my electric toothbrush, going through the motions. The routine felt weird, without my son standing on his little step stool next to me, mimicking everything I did, asking a million questions about why we had to brush our tongues and wash behind our ears.

I missed him so much.

So I *FaceTimed* him, needing to see his face, needing to hear his voice, needing to know he was okay even though I knew he was fine.

"Hi, mommy! I'm brushing my teeth, wook!" he said as soon as his little face filled the screen, his mouth full of toothpaste foam.

"Good morning, son! I see! Good job!" I said, smiling despite the ache in my chest, despite the tears I wanted to cry.

I watched as he brushed his teeth like a big boy, doing it all by himself, not needing me to help. I was so proud of him, so amazed at how independent he was becoming. But also sad seeing that maybe he didn't need my help so much after all. That he was growing up. That one day he wouldn't need me at all.

"Your tongue too, papa!" I reminded him, because he always forgot that part.

He stuck out his tongue and scrubbed it with his toothbrush, making funny faces.

Soon after, I heard a female voice in the background say, "Savy, are you almost done?"

And he yelled out, "Yessss!"

My stomach clenched. Sena. In the bathroom with my son. Doing my morning routine with my baby.

I bet Sena would love nothing more than to replace me. It seemed like a genuine desire on her part, not just to be with Sacavè, but to be Saviour's mother. To take everything I had and make it hers.

"Let's do your affirmations, baby," I said, needing that connection to my son.

"Okay! I am smart. I am kind. I am a warrior of light. I am happy today, tomorrow, and forever," he recited perfectly.

My heart swelled with pride and love.

"That's right, baby. I love you. Have a good day at school, okay?" I said.

"Yes, mommy. I love you, okay!" he said.

"Where's TT Sena?" I asked.

"Right here," Saviour said, moving his little hands to pick up the iPad and turn it toward the doorway, showing Sena standing there, her hair wrapped, looking comfortable and at home.

One thing my child was going to do was tell the whole truth. He didn't know about secrets or protecting people's feelings. He just showed me exactly what I asked to see.

"Okay, see you after school, okay?" I said.

"Not daddy and TT Sena like last time?" he asked, his little face scrunched up in confusion about the pickup routine.

"No, papa. I'll be there. Look for mommy's truck. Give me besos," I said.

He kissed all over the screen.

I made a mental note to never miss another morning regimen with my baby. Never let another woman take my place in his routine. Never let work or exhaustion or my own bullshit keep me from these moments.

"Okay, see you later," I said, tears falling freely now that he couldn't see my face clearly through his kisses on the screen.

"Bye-bye!" he said, tapping the red button to hang up before I could say anything else.

That triggered my separation anxiety so terribly. All I wanted was to get in my car, drive to Sacavè's house, and get my baby right then. Let him play hooky for the day. Keep him with me where he belonged.

"Oh God, please keep him young and innocent forever," I whispered to myself.

***

"Nice to see you, Mrs. Sanders. Or should I say Miss Williams?" my attorney said as he walked into his office, a manila folder in his hands, a slight smile on his professional face.

"Please, have a seat."

I gave him a half smile because that's truly how I felt, half here, half somewhere else. He finally signed, and I should be happy. Should be celebrating. Should be popping bottles and dancing around my living room. I had waited for this moment for almost a year.

But I still felt like a failure.

Years ago, all I wanted was to be this man's wife. To walk down an aisle in a white dress with my father, if he'd been in my life, giving me away. To have bridesmaids in matching dresses standing beside me. To toss the bouquet to the single ladies, laughing and celebrating love. To wash his feet in a bowl of water to show my submission on our wedding night like my grandmother had done for my grandfather. To have a honeymoon somewhere tropical like Jamaica or the Bahamas or anywhere with clear blue water and white sand.

Instead, I got a damn courthouse wedding on a random Thursday afternoon with Sena as our only witness. No dress. No flowers. No celebration. Just paperwork and a judge who looked bored out of his mind, running through the ceremony like he had ten more to do that day.

And here I am, sitting in this attorney's office, still sad as hell that it's about to be over. Sad for what I had convinced myself could've been if he'd just tried harder. Sad for my son, who would grow up in a broken home like I did.

"Okay, perfect," my attorney said, flipping through the papers I had brought. "I actually have to submit this to the court clerk, and then there's a mandatory waiting period. After that, assuming no one contests it, the divorce will be finalized and you'll receive your decree in the mail."

He continued explaining the timeline, what to expect, what could potentially hold things up, what I should do if Sacavè changed his mind. I nodded along, trying to focus, trying to absorb the information.

"Do you have any questions?" he asked, looking at me over his reading glasses.

All I could say was, "Thank you so much for your patience," like I was clocked in at work and addressing a customer instead of discussing the end of my marriage.

The whole ride back home, all I could think about was finally being a free agent. No more being tied to Sacavè. No more awkward conversations about my marital status. No more lying on forms that asked if I was married or single.

Then my mind went to Tool.

This was everything he wanted, right? He needed me divorced to pursue me. To make me his. To give me his last name like he'd promised that first day at the QuikTrip. He'd been patient, had set boundaries, had walked away when I couldn't give him what he needed.

And his moment was finally here.

I got home with thirty minutes to spare before I needed to clock in for my remote work shift, so I made myself a bacon, egg, and cheese bagel and some coffee, my comfort meal. I sat at my kitchen island, contemplating what I should say to Tool.

He was pretty straight cut, so I didn't want to beat around the bush. Didn't want to play games or make him guess.

He'd been clear about what he wanted. Now I could give it to him.

I decided to text him: *He signed the papers.*

No good morning. No "hey, handsome." No preamble. Straight cut.

I stared at my phone, at those four words, my thumb hovering over the send button. This felt bigger than just a text. This felt like I was closing one door and opening another. Like I was making a choice I couldn't take back.

I hit *send.*

Then, before I could change my mind, I added: *I'm practically divorced. So come get me. No reneging.*

My heart was pounding as I watched the "delivered" notification pop up, then the three dots that meant he was typing. Then they disappeared. Then appeared again. He was thinking about what to say. Probably shocked.

I took a bite of my bagel even though I had lost my appetite, waiting for his response.

***

Working from home was kicking my ass more than I thought it would. I thought I would've been so full of energy since I wasn't commuting an hour each way through Atlanta traffic. I imagined myself in cute loungewear, sipping coffee, knocking out my work in half the time, having energy left to be a better version of myself.

But I was still beat. More tired than I had been working in the office, actually.

The isolation was getting to me. The lack of structure. The way work and home blurred together until I couldn't tell where one ended and the other began. And I couldn't even utilize my lunch break to take a quick twenty-minute nap like I had planned because I needed to use it to pick up my son from school instead.

I had more energy working from the office, honestly, with Myra and Eric making me laugh, when I was forced to get dressed and leave the house. I could use a triple espresso iced caramel macchiato right about now. Mental note: add an espresso machine to my Amazon cart. Maybe that would help.

On the upside, me and Tool had been texting all morning. Non-stop, actually. My phone kept lighting up with his name, making me smile despite everything else going on.

He started out consoling me, like he could read between the lines of my text. His first message back asked me how I felt about the divorce being filed. He let me know that I wasn't a failure as long as I felt like I did my part as a wife.

That maybe everything happened for a reason. That perhaps Sacavè wasn't my perfect husband, but he was. And it was meant for us to meet at that gas station three months ago, at that exact moment, at that exact QuikTrip.

When I tell you I had to mute my work call to bust out laughing at that message? The confidence. The certainty. The way he just claimed me like it was already decided.

It definitely lightened the mood not only between us, but my overall mental state. I had been spiraling all morning, drowning in sadness and anxiety about the future. And here he was, pulling me out of it with a single text.

The topic of divorce was short-lived. We started making plans for dates and trips, all in the same conversation. He wanted to take a trip to Puerto Rico to celebrate my promotion and my divorce, a fresh start, he called it. A new chapter. Sun, sand, and rum.

But I mentioned my son's birthday being a couple of weeks away, Saviour would be turning five, and I couldn't miss that, couldn't be gone for his birthday. I had already missed too many moments this week.

He said he'd look at dates three weeks out instead, no hesitation, no complaint. Just immediate accommodation. Just understanding that my son came first, always.

So I was getting my all-expenses-paid trip after all. Puerto Rico. With a man who wanted me. Who chose me. Who was willing to wait for me.

He tried to include Saviour in the plans too, suggested we make it a family trip, that he'd book a suite with separate rooms, that Saviour would love the beach and the swimming pools. But honestly, I felt like it would be a little too soon for that. Saviour had met Tool one time prior as "mommy's friend" in the driveway for all of five minutes. A vacation all together, sharing space, playing family? That was pushing it. That was moving too fast for my son, even if I was ready.

I needed to establish what Tool and I were first. Needed to make sure this was real and lasting before I brought my baby into it. Because if it didn't work out, if Tool turned out to be like all the others, I didn't want Saviour getting attached and then losing another man in his life.

**

My lunch break came, and I went to pick up my son from school.

I realized immediately that he didn't have his iPad with him.

165

I didn't want to reach out to Sacavè because I was obviously being avoided at this point. Not only that, but the thought of Sena holding onto my child's iPad made me want to cut the fuck up.

Every morning, faithfully, I leave my son's iPad with his teacher, Miss Marie. I know he'd want it when going with his dad after school. His teacher was okay with it as long as Saviour never expected to play with it during class.

Sena had already crossed the line getting my number from his iPad. Now she felt the need to hold onto it. But why?

Saviour wouldn't have allowed her to forget that Miss Marie was supposed to get his iPad either. So keeping it had been intentional.

When I asked him where it was, he said, "TT Sena said it will be at daddy's house and that I don't need it all the time."

I wanted to say, "Well, your dad needs to get one that stays at his house then. And what the fuck does she mean you don't need it all the time?"

He doesn't have it all the time. First of all, I promised myself I wouldn't be an "electronic mom." Using his iPad is often served as a reward. He reads. He plays with his toys and blocks. He plays outside too.

I'm starting to feel more and more like this bitch is testing me.

I would've called her now that she had my number, but that would give her too much satisfaction. So I texted Sacavè instead: *Where's my son's iPad?*

He responded: *It must be in Sena's car.*

The fact that he wasn't sure and she told my son it would be at his dad's house irritated me even more. But there was nothing I could do about it right then. My lunch break was over, and it was time to get back to work.

I texted him back: *Can you drop it off please?*

And that was that.

If Sena was around for the long haul, I had to get used to her new position as my son's stepmom. But the weird shit had to stop.

It was one thing if maybe she didn't know I usually left it with the teacher. But let my son tell it, she'd been with his dad to pick him up before. So she knew. And her weird-ass comment about "all the time" told me her intentions.

It's not something I'm going to address with Sacavè right now because he knows how I feel about her, and I don't want it to come off as jealousy.

So I'll nip it in the bud with her if it becomes necessary. Simple.

Chapter 15

2 Weeks Later

Sacavè and I had been good at avoiding each other until now. Because Saviour's party was today, and there was no avoiding him at the party.

Every time in the past two weeks that he'd come over to see Saviour or even bring him food, I had been conveniently clocked in and taking calls, keeping our interactions minimal. The longest conversation we'd had since I got those papers was a text exchange where he expressed how he didn't appreciate the new pickup schedule. He felt like he'd started to see our son less.

So, to compromise, we went back to him doing the after-school pickup. It gave him more time with Saviour, and honestly, it gave me more time to work uninterrupted. Win-win.

I guess I can say I didn't know he was going to let the divorce be such a breeze. No fighting. No drama. No last-minute attempts to change my mind. Just . . . cooperation. It was almost unsettling how easy he was making this.

Either way, I had invited Tool and his niece and nephew to my son's party too. I'm a little nervous about it because it'll be his first time around my family, my mom, my sister, my cousins, all of them. And they could be a lot. I had to make sure I warned them to be on their best behavior, especially in case Sena decided to show her face too. I didn't put it past her to show up, claiming she was "Saviour's godmother" and had every right to be there.

My son wanted a NASCAR-themed party, so we threw it at K1 Speed, the indoor go-kart place that Saviour had been begging to visit for months. My friends brought their kids, some of his friends from school showed up, and his cousins all came through. The venue provided everything: racing suits for the kids, a meet-and-greet with a "professional driver" who was really just an employee in a jumpsuit, and of course, the go-kart rides that made all the kids feel like real racers.

Just as we were about to sing "Happy Birthday," I noticed Tool walking in with two young kids, a little girl who looked about five and a boy who looked about seven, all three of them holding gift bags wrapped in shiny NASCAR paper.

He was so late. The kids had already missed the meet-and-greet and the first round of car rides. But he was here, and that's what mattered.

I waved him over to the table as we started to sing "Happy Birthday," and I could see Sacavè's face change from my peripheral vision. His jaw tightened. His whole body went stiff. Maybe because he'd assumed Tool wouldn't come. Maybe because he hadn't brought Sena but I had brought my new man. Either way, it was neither here nor there for me anymore. This was about Saviour, not about Sacavè's feelings.

When the singing was over and Saviour blew out his candles, all five of them, plus one for good luck, Sacavè gave me the stare of death.

But of course, I ignored him.

What's crazy is that his best friend Sena being at every family function for the past four years was never an issue. She was at every birthday, every holiday, every celebration. But now someone I'm dating shows up, and I'm getting dirty side eyes? The hypocrisy was laughable.

Don't get me wrong, I didn't invite Tool to intentionally be petty. Tool offered to come and bring his niece and nephew so they could play with other kids, and I agreed.

Nothing and no one was going to ruin my baby's party. Hell, if his dad had an issue with anything, he could leave too. I didn't care what he'd contributed financially. I was fully capable of throwing this party on my own.

My mom and my sister had started to cut and serve the cake, Miss Sheila's famous red velvet cake that everyone always requested, and I walked over to Tool and the kids.

"Hey, pretty girl," I said, greeting his niece.

"Hey, handsome," I said to his nephew, giving him a high-five.

"Hey, big handsome," I said to Tool, greeting him with a smile that was probably too big, too obvious. But then I had to keep it cute with a church hug.

"What's up, beautiful? This is Nala and BJ," Tool said, pointing to his niece and nephew.

Nala favored him a lot, same nose, same smile, same energy. His side of the family had to have some strong genes, or maybe he'd pissed his sister off a lot during her pregnancy and the baby came out looking just like him as punishment.

My son ran over to me with my mama on his tail, quickly greeting Tool with a "Hi, Tool! I really like my truck!" followed by a quick hug before returning to me and saying, "Mommy, Suga said come ask you if you want cake."

Suga was what he called my mama. He had been calling her that since he could talk.

"No, baby, mommy needs to lay off the cake," I said back, patting my stomach that had gotten noticeably thicker in the past two weeks.

Between working from home with little to no movement, no walking to meetings, no walking to my car, no walking anywhere really, and Tool taking me to new restaurants every other day, trying every restaurant Atlanta had to offer, I had gained eight pounds. My jeans were tighter. My face was fuller. I could see it in pictures.

Although Miss Sheila made the best red velvet cake in the city, I'd have to pass.

My mother came and stood behind Saviour with her hands on his shoulders, as if she was waiting on an introduction. My sister and my cousin came walking over too, curiosity written all over their faces.

"Tevin, this is my mom, Tonya. My sister Tamia, and my favorite cousin Ness," I said, gesturing to each of them. "Y'all, this is Tool. And his niece and nephew, Nala and BJ."

The kids waved politely. My mama, never one to be formal, went to reach out her hand to shake Tool's hand, but he said, "Come on, mama. I'm a hugger," and pulled her in for a hug.

Then he reached out to hug Tamia and Ness too then he high-fived Saviour, who was bouncing with excitement at all the attention.

"Mama, I see where she gets it from now," Tool said to my mom, charming her already.

"Come on, Saviour. Let's go get Nala and BJ some cake," I said, needing to give Tool space to talk to my family without me hovering.

Tool paused his conversation with my mom. "Hold on, mama. You too. Ain't nothing wrong with you. Eat some cake," he said, his voice playful but insistent.

As I was cutting more cake slices, carefully portioning them out on NASCAR-themed paper plates, I looked over to see Tool deep in conversation with my mama, my sister, and Ness. They were laughing, carrying on, completely at ease with him.

I wanted Saviour to open all his gifts while we were still at the party. The table was packed with presents but we didn't have the venue reserved for much longer. So I started passing out the goodie bags to all the kids, then packed up the leftover cake and food while Sacavè, without me asking, loaded Saviour's gifts into my truck.

All the kids went off to play one last round in the arcade area, burning off their sugar highs. Tool had finally broken away from my mama, who'd probably grilled him with a thousand questions, and walked over behind me.

"So, what do you need help with?" he asked, standing close enough that I could smell his cologne.

I looked around. Honestly, there was nothing left to do. The venue staff had already stripped the tables, dumped the trash, wiped down surfaces. Everything else I would've asked Sacavè to help with, but he was already handling the gifts.

"I think we're good," I said. "But thank you."

I don't know if Sacavè being around was making Tool feel like he needed to prove something, but there was a tension in the air, this unspoken competition between two men who both cared about me and my son in different ways.

Here's the thing: Tool and I had a trip already booked. Puerto Rico. PTO approved. We were leaving in eleven days. But I hadn't said a word about that to Sacavè yet. Hadn't mentioned it. Hadn't prepared him for the fact that I had to be gone, that he'd have Saviour for five whole days, that I was moving on with my life in very real, very permanent ways.

I wanted to avoid conflict at all costs. Initially, I had a fuzzy headspace about the divorce . . . grief, confusion, second-guessing. But now I was clear. I was ready. I wasn't sure where Sacavè's head was at though. He hadn't mentioned the divorce once. Neither had I.

I hate leaving things unsaid, sweeping problems under the rug. But that was Sacavè's specialty, he would just sit with shit, let it fester, until one day he exploded. So he could sit with this until he decided to say something.

My mom was my backup plan if he gave me pushback about the trip. She'd already agreed to be on standby in case Sacavè couldn't handle the full five days alone.

Tool started telling me everything my mom had asked him, laughing about her interrogation about where he worked, where he grew up, what his intentions were with me, if he had any kids, what his relationship with God looked like. All the questions a protective mother asks when her daughter brings a man around for the first time.

We were standing there talking, laughing, the venue staff cleaning up around us, when Sacavè walked back in from loading the last of the gifts.

Tool, ever confident, jumped up and said, "Aye, man, if you want my help, I gotcha, bra."

I loved that Tool was willing to exist in my world and Sacavè's world simultaneously. His confidence, his demeanor, basically said: if anyone's going to be uncomfortable here, it won't be me.

Sacavè looked up, sized Tool up for a second, then said, "Nah, man. I'm cool. Appreciate it though."

Then he looked over to me and said, "Ki, whatever can't fit in your truck, I'll put in mine."

I nodded, grateful that they were being civil, that my son didn't have to witness any drama on his birthday.

***

"Savy, did you enjoy your party?" I asked as we got home and he started tearing into all his unopened gifts, ripping paper and tossing bows aside.

"Yes, mommy!" he said, his face lit up with pure joy.

My child was blessed beyond measure, and I was grateful for my village. Between my family, his dad's family, our friends, and even Tool's contribution, Saviour had more toys and clothes than he knew what to do with.

Being that it was the weekend, he was supposed to go with his dad after his party like we'd planned. But he'd asked to stay with me instead. Honestly, he just wanted to open his gifts.

I tried to convince him by saying they would all be here when he got back, or that he could take some and unwrap them at his dad's house. But he'd gotten so frustrated at the suggestion that he started to cry.

His dad looked hurt about it too. I could see it in his face, the disappointment, the rejection. I assumed he had something at his house planned, maybe a surprise or a special gift he wanted to give Saviour alone.

"I'll just drop him off tomorrow," I mouthed to Sacavè.

He just nodded, his jaw tight, and continued unloading his new Durango. This was my first time seeing it, the *biborce* that my son had been telling me about all week.

"It's nice," I said, genuinely impressed. The Durango was clean, fully loaded, clearly expensive.

"Why'd you get a new truck? You must be expanding your family."

I couldn't help but crack a joke to break the tension.

"You must be expanding yours. You're gaining weight," he responded immediately.

Oop.

I'm shocked that he even said that. Clearly, he wasn't in a joking mood with me because he took it there, went straight for the dome.

He finished unloading the last box, said his goodbyes to our son with a long hug and kisses on his forehead, then left without another word to me.

177

I gotta admit, he hadn't been himself lately. The overtime hours at work. The willingness to sign the papers without a fight. The standoffish energy. The uptightness. Something seemed off, even in the way he'd maturely interacted with Tool, no confrontation, no territorial behavior, no jealousy.

Even the way he didn't express obvious disapproval about Tool being at the party was weird. All of it was just unlike him.

On second thought, maybe this was what detached and divorced co-parenting felt like. Polite. Distant. Civil. I mean, I still wanted my friend out of the deal, wanted the version of Sacavè who used to make me laugh, who I could talk to about anything. But I guess that choice isn't mine anymore.

"Ooooh!" Saviour yelled out, snapping me out of my thoughts as he unwrapped a remote-control car.

I walked over and sat Indian-style beside him on the living room floor, folding gift bags and opening cards while he focused solely on the toys. He'd thrown all the cards and clothes to the side immediately, too young to realize that's where the best gifts were, tucked inside those envelopes.

I had wanted him to open them one by one so he knew who gave him what, so he could thank people accordingly. But he was already several gifts in, creating chaos and wrapping paper carnage everywhere.

This felt so rich, making birthday memories with my son. Because I don't remember any of mine as a kid. No parties. No gifts piled high. No family gatherings centered around celebrating me.

I was determined to give Saviour something different. Something better.

By the time Saviour finished opening everything, he'd accumulated $500 in cash from various relatives, $100 in V-Bucks for his games, and clothes, shoes, and toys.

Now it was time to whine down. Bath time. Bedtime.

As I put him in the bath, scrubbing behind his ears while he played with his bath toys and recounted every detail of his party, I heard a ding from my phone in the other room.

A text message from Tool: *Bae, call me when you can.*

It would be a minute before I actually called him back because I wanted to be settled first. Needed to finish Saviour's bath, get him in his pajamas, read him a bedtime story, tuck him in, take my own bath, and decompress from the day.

An hour later, finally in my own bed, hair wrapped, face washed, body exhausted, I called him.

"Hey, baby," I said as soon as he answered.

"What's going on, baby girl?" he said, his voice groggy like he'd been asleep.

I wouldn't be surprised if he had been. I was worn out from the party too, the planning, the executing, the socializing. Then the gift opening chaos, the cleanup, the bath routine, the bedtime story, my own bath and unwinding. I was running on fumes.

"Baby, I'm exhausted. Were you sleeping?" I asked.

"Almost," he said. "Nala and BJ tore me up today, but they had so much fun. I just wanted to tell you thank you for inviting us and say goodnight."

His voice was soft, genuine, appreciative.

"No problem. Thank you all for coming and for the gifts too. Goodnight," I said, smiling.

Everything about today felt right, felt aligned, felt like progress. And I was grateful.

So fucking grateful.

Chapter 16

Sacavè woke me up at the ass crack of dawn to bring Saviour over. When I suggested we let him wake up naturally because he was likely exhausted from the party yesterday, the inconsiderate ass nigga gave me pushback. Apparently, whatever he had planned just couldn't wait for our son to wake up on his own. Like the world would end if Saviour slept past 8 AM on a Sunday.

If I had known I wasn't going to have the luxury of sleeping in either, I promise you my son would've taken his ass over there last night. But after my twenty-minute attempt at waking him up for what he knew wasn't a school day, with the reason being "to go to daddy's," all I got was tears. Fat, dramatic tears rolling down his little face like I was torturing him.

The ice cream bribe got old when they started selling the SpongeBob popsicles with the bubblegum eyes in the big boxes in the freezer section at Costco. Now he had a whole stash in our freezer. No incentive power anymore. So his dad could deal with the wake-up battle when he got here.

I called on Sacavè when I had trouble getting our son up and ready, even on school days. But for some reason, I just felt like he was taking this one out of proportion. Making a big deal out of nothing. Being difficult for the sake of being difficult.

I am simply not one of those parents who will force or whoop my child if he doesn't want to go somewhere. Because you never know the reason a child doesn't want to go. They're humans too, with feelings and preferences and bad days. And there are many times I don't want to go somewhere either, I just have to adult through it. But Saviour? He's five. He doesn't have to.

Saviour adores his dad. The mention of him usually gets him right up out of bed, especially the mention of going to his house where there aren't as many rules. No "wash your hands before you eat." No "clean up your toys before you get new ones out." Just chaos, fun and daddy energy.

Last night, I understood him being excited about opening his birthday gifts. That made sense. But today? I didn't know what the resistance was about. He goes to his dad's every weekend, so trust me, it's not because I made plans that would interfere with his time.

In fact, to make it easier on Sacavè when he got here, I had already picked out an outfit and shoes for Saviour and laid them out on the dresser. And I had started breakfast to make sure he ate before they left, French toast sticks and sausages in the air fryer, his favorite.

Of course, Sacavè got here and without even as much as a "good morning", no acknowledgment that I existed, went straight upstairs to Saviour's room.

And wouldn't you know it, Saviour got right on up for his dad like it was nothing. Like he hadn't just been crying and refusing to move ten minutes ago. He brushed his teeth and got dressed with ease, then came down the stairs with his face already greased up and smiling.

It was in that moment I realized I'm raising a little manipulator. A little con artist who knew exactly how to play both his parents.

I pulled his French toast sticks and sausages out of the air fryer, plated his food, poured his apple juice, and set out his gummy vitamins. Then I got out of the way and let his dad have him.

Sacavè sat at the table with Saviour while he ate, talking to him about their plans for the day. I overheard him mention that he, Saviour, and TT Sena were going to a place called

Malibu Grand Prix to ride bumper cars and play arcade games.

Sacavè was still being distant with me. We had a typical interaction about him having his shoes on my carpet, but that was it. No real conversation. No eye contact. Just functional co-parenting at its most basic level.

Finally, I decided to just rip the Band-Aid off. "Can I talk to you real quick?" I asked.

Without answering me, without even looking at me, he instructed our son: "Savy, go upstairs and get your shoes and iPad."

When Saviour's little feet took off up the stairs, I said, "So I just wanted to let you know that in ten days, I'll be going out of town for five days."

"By yourself?" he asked.

I choked a little bit on my words because . . . *nigga, you're Saviour's daddy, not mine. Why are you questioning me like you have a right to know my business?*

"What do you mean 'by myself'? Our son will not be going, no," I answered back.

"Okay, bet," he said dryly, bending down to put on his shoes.

Then he added, without looking up: "Keep that nigga from around my son. He got a daddy."

184

And then he walked out the door before I could respond. Before I could tell him about himself. Before I could remind him of his hypocrisy.

I guess it's fair to say he's back to himself. The detached, cooperative Sacavè of the past two weeks? Gone. The petty, controlling, hypocritical Sacavè? Back in full force.

"And he has a step daddy too, bitter ass nigga," I mumbled.

It's crazy how men have these double standards about everything. He was about to take my son out with his side bitch bestie and hadn't run it by me at all. And I'm over here not being bitter about it, not making comments, not demanding he keep her away from our child. But I mention going on a trip not even mentioning Tool specifically and suddenly he's got rules, boundaries and demands?

Saviour came running down the stairs with his iPad and one of his new trucks from yesterday, ready to go.

"Have fun, papa!" I yelled out as he ran to his dad's truck.

"Bye, mommy! Love you!" he yelled back, already climbing into his car seat.

I decided to call my sister to vent because I honestly felt irritated about everything after they left. Like something was building inside me that I couldn't keep suppressed much longer.

I should've said it all to him, should've checked him right there in my living room, should've told him exactly where he could put his double standards. But I had been trying to keep the peace. Trying to be the bigger person. Trying to make co-parenting work.

I felt like I had been suppressing everything since the day I opened that envelope. From Sena answering his phone to him not returning my call. The iPad situation. Us avoiding each other up until our son's party. Him being distant and not talkative. And now this comment about Tool being around our son.

As much as I hated how things turned out with Sena, the fact that they ended up together after denying it for so long, I had never once told him that I didn't want her around Saviour. Never made demands. Never set boundaries like he was trying to do with Tool.

Although she's the reason we're no longer together, I had kept my mouth shut and my opinions to myself because I knew she treated Saviour well. And that's what mattered.

Men have this level of selfishness. They will not bend or break. Women always compromise. Always sacrifice.

All I can say is: be careful who you marry. And most importantly, be careful who you have a baby with.

My heartbreak doesn't come from having a divorce. It comes from everything I dealt with and settled for during the entire relationship. Looking back, at the rate things were going, we should've never gotten married in the first place.

This was my breaking point. The point during a divorce where the wife starts wanting alimony, not that money should compensate for emotional damage, but nigga, pay me for all you put me through. Oh, and child support for bringing my child into this shit. The point where you only want supervised visits with your child because that pure spirit doesn't deserve to be around your toxic energy. The point where everyone who's never been in your situation calls you bitter.

To me, I'm not bitter. I'm just done.

"Hello?" Tamia answered on the second ring.

"Girl," I said, and she already knew from my tone that I needed to vent.

I told her everything. The early morning wake-up call. Sacavè's attitude. The comment about Tool. The hypocrisy of him taking Saviour around Sena without asking but demanding I keep Tool away.

"Sista, just be happy he signed it and didn't decide to be a deadbeat after. A win is a win," Tamia said sounding practical.

And honestly, that was one way to look at it. A better way to look at it. She was right. I could be dealing with so much worse. He could've abandoned Saviour out of spite. He could've fought the divorce and dragged me through court for years. He could've made my life hell.

Instead, he signed the papers and remained an active father. That was something.

"True," I said.

"And fuck him, sista. Think about that trip to San Juan with that man! Gworl, Sacavè never took you anywhere but to the clinic for STD tests and the courthouse to sign papers," Tamia said, making me burst out laughing despite my mood.

She wasn't lying. Thirteen years together, nine years dating, four years married, and we'd never been on a vacation. Never been on a trip. Never been anywhere that required a plane ticket, a passport or planning more than a week out.

The most romantic thing he'd ever done was take me to Pappadeaux for my birthday.

"Sistaaa, clock it! I'm so excited! My bathing suits and outfits are tea!" I said, my mood lifting as I thought about the trip.

We spent the next two hours on the phone chatting about everything San Juan, outfits, excursions, restaurants, beaches, what I should pack and what shoes to bring.

Until Tamia said, "You gonna finally give that man some pumpum, sista?"

I froze.

That was the last thing on my mind, honestly. For some reason, sex with Tool was nothing I had thought about in concrete terms. Of course, some pussy was deserved, the man had been patient, respectful, had set boundaries and stuck to them. But was he going to be on some bullshit like he was before? The whole "I don't fuck married women" thing?

The anxiety hit me all at once. I didn't even know if the room we'd booked at the Condado Vanderbilt had one bed or two. We'd booked it together over the phone, but I hadn't paid attention to those details. I had just been excited about the trip itself.

What if he booked two beds? What if he still wasn't ready?

"You know I am, sista," I answered, trying to sound confident even though my stomach was in knots.

"Mmhmm, you sound scary," Tamia said, laughing at me.

"I'm not scary! I'm just . . . I don't know. What if he's still on that 'I can't' type shit?" I admitted.

"Girl, the papers are filed. You're basically divorced. If that man don't give you some dick in Puerto Rico after all this, then he might be gay and need you as his cover up," Tamia said.

"You right," I said, feeling a little better.

"And even if he don't, there's plenty of fine Puerto Rican men on that island who will," Tamia added, making us both crack up.

She had a point.

By the time we hung up, I felt lighter. Less burdened. Ready to focus on the trip instead of Sacavè's bullshit.

Chapter 17

"Hello Ms. Williams to be its Mark Rosenbaum just calling to let you know that our little problem is no longer a problem and everything has been filed in court" the voicemail said.

I was ecstatic to hear it. I felt like I was holding my breath for two days now. A couple days ago, my attorney called and said there were a few discrepancies within the paperwork that had me a little nervous thinking that the biggest discrepancy might've changed his mind. I hadn't mentioned that part to Tool though. I didn't want radio silence between us again. I felt like I won the lottery or something. It was such a relief. My attorney warned me it would be at least six months before everything was finalized. Georgia didn't play when it came to divorce timelines, but just knowing the process had officially started was enough for me.

This is the perfect Friday surprise to start off my vacation week. I would've hated to be in PR celebrating a divorce that wasn't even in progress. This was the beginning I knew I had a while before it was final, but starting to process felt like freedom was finally within reach. I dailed Tool.

"Sooo I was thinking, how about you come spend the weekend with me?" I asked nervously.

"Most definitely," he answered without hesitation. "When I get off I'll go home, shower and pack a bag and be over there!"

That was actually smoother than I thought. After all our trip was 5 days away.

***

It was my office day, and boy was I ready to get off. Today was my first time seeing Trey since we had sex again, and honestly, I was content with the days we walked past each other like complete strangers. I know that bruised his ego, but I'm grown. My days of being dickmatized were over. My future ex-husband burned that bridge, so yeah, I'd reminisce when I seen Trey's pigeon-toed ass walking by, but Miss Loofah could have that.

"What's up, Kia?" Trey greeted as he walked by.

"Hello, Trey," I returned, practically skipping to my desk.

"Hold up," he said, trying to keep up. "You look good."

"Thank you. I like pink like the loofah on your showerhead," I whispered the last part.

He looked shocked that I even said that. I was in a good mood, and I was bound to say whatever the fuck I wanted to say. He seemed to be at a loss for words, so I started to walk off until he grabbed my arm. I instantly started looking around to see if anyone else noticed before I snatched my arm back.

"Wait, so that's why you left?" Trey asked, then started laughing. "That's my shit! CVS only had pink and purple, and a nigga needed a loofah. I guess I should've went with purple."

"Or went to Target," I said as I kept walking.

I'm sure he wasn't lying. I'd like to believe niggas were sneakier than that these days, but I had no reason to give him the benefit of the doubt. And honestly, the loofah was one of many reasons I was done with Trey. He was too short. He drove a loud ass Scat Pack, which meant he loved attention. And he'd been single as long as I'd been at Sertec. Like, if no one wanted you in all that time, that told me something.

As soon as I got to my desk, my watch went off with a text from Trey: *Target isn't 24 hours.*

That was funny, but it was still a hard pass for me. The dick didn't come with dates, just dick and DoorDash. I was currently digging my standards out of the pits of hell, and that just didn't cut it anymore.

***

The end of the workday was here, and I couldn't wait to get home and get my house ready for my man. This would be the first time he was actually coming inside and staying. I was loading my bag into the car when I heard a chime from my phone. I just knew it was Tool, but when I looked down, my stomach dropped.

It was Sacavè with a text message: *Call me ASAP.*

He had Saviour, so that made me panic. I dropped everything on the front seat and called immediately.

As soon as he answered, his voice was sharp. "So you forged my signature on the divorce papers?"

"Nigga, I did what?" I said, genuinely confused.

"Now you acting confused. It's cool. I'll take yo' ass to court," he said before hanging up.

I stared at my phone, pissed. What the fuck was he talking about? I didn't forge shit. My attorney filed the papers I signed and gave Sacavè to sign. If anything, he was probably dodging the process like he always did, and now he was trying to blame me for it.

I called back a couple of times, but he didn't answer. More power to him, because I was going about my day. I would've gone to celebrate with a couple espresso martinis if I didn't have to get my house ready for my man.

I wasn't letting his ass ruin my mood. Not today.

***

"Do you know what you want for dinner?" I asked Tool over the phone.

They'd worked him for three extra hours, so I decided to cook for us instead of going out.

"Steak or lamb chops and potatoes with broccolini," he said. "I'm 'bout to get the groceries delivered while I go to my spot and get ready. What else you need? You got enough Taylor Port?"

I laughed because that's all I'd been talking about lately. "Yes, I have enough Taylor Port, baby. But I can go to the store and get the stuff."

"They gon' be there by the time you get out the shower, Kia," he said, a little annoyed.

He had already told me I frustrated him with that. I knew my love language was acts of service, but every time he tried to do something for me, I'd try to talk him out of it. He didn't understand it was a defense mechanism, a reaction to Sacavè that I was trying to unlearn. But I appreciated his effort.

"Okay, baby. Thank you," I said softly.

"That's better," he said, and I could hear the smile in his voice.

***

As soon as I got out the shower, the doorbell rang. I hadn't seen anyone on the camera, so I figured it was the grocery delivery. I wrapped up in my robe and ran downstairs to grab the bags, then decided I'd unload and prep the food while I was already in the kitchen.

He went with lamb chops, so I cleaned and seasoned them with garlic, rosemary, and a little cayenne pepper for some spice, then set them in the fridge to marinate. I repeated the process with the potatoes, cutting them into wedges, tossing them in olive oil, salt, pepper, and paprika before sliding them into the oven since they'd take the longest. The broccolini was new for me. I'd cooked broccoli before, but broccolini looked like a mix of broccoli and asparagus, so I decided to cook it like I would asparagus. I laid them on a pan, drizzled them with avocado oil, and sprinkled on my seasoning.

As soon as I slid the pan into the oven, I heard Tool's truck rumbling in the driveway. I opened the garage instead of answering the door, but the little girl in me was so nervous. To make matters worse, I hadn't made it back upstairs to lotion up or change into something cute. I was still in my robe with my hair tied up in a silk scarf, looking a whole mess.

"Hey, beautiful," Tool said, stepping inside and handing me my usual bouquet of pink flowers. He'd started giving me a vase each time because he brought me flowers so frequently that the old ones never had time to die before he was replacing them.

"Hey, babe. Sorry I jumped out the shower right in time for the groceries. I was trying to get everything prepped before you came. I didn't have time to get dressed," I explained.

He grabbed my waist and started kissing me, his Nike gym bag still across his body and the flowers in his hand. "My day was great. What about yours?" he said sarcastically.

I laughed.

"Stop explaining yourself so much, woman. Grab these," he said, handing me the flowers.

Explaining everything was another habit I had. Tool joked that Sacavè must've been strict because I always had a reason for everything I did. Every time I'd start to explain, he'd say, "This ain't boot camp, baby. This is Love Island." We'd both laugh.

"Okay, come on. Let me give you the official tour," I said, grabbing his hand.

***

I showed him everything, the living room with the big windows that let in all the natural light, the kitchen where I spent most of my time experimenting with new recipes, my bedroom with the plush king-sized bed and soft gray comforter that felt like sleeping on a cloud, and even Saviour's room with all his toys still scattered around from this morning's play session.

"That was nice, Kia. Real nice," Tool said, wrapping his arms around me from behind as we stood in my bedroom. "You did good, baby."

"Thank you," I said, leaning back into him. It felt good to have him here, in my space. This was mine, something I'd built after everything fell apart.

We walked back downstairs, and I checked on the food. The smell of roasted potatoes and seasoned lamb filled the kitchen, making my stomach growl. Everything was coming together perfectly. Tool sat at the island, watching me move around the kitchen with an intensity that made me blush.

"You look so comfortable," he said.

"I am," I said, smiling at him. "This is my happy place."

"Nah," he said, standing up and walking over to me. "I'm your happy place."

He wasn't lying.

***

I turned the stove off and started plating our food. Tool stayed close, his hands finding my waist every time I moved past him. The kitchen felt smaller with him in it, but in the best way possible.

"Go sit down," I said, shooing him toward the table. "Let me bring this out."

"You sure?" he asked, but he was already heading to the dining room.

I carried both plates over, setting his down first before taking my seat across from him. He was already eyeing the food like he hadn't eaten all day.

"Damn, this looks good," he said, picking up his fork.

"Well, don't just look at it," I said, laughing. "Taste it."

***

Dinner was perfect. The lamb chops were tender and flavorful, the potatoes crispy on the outside and fluffy on the inside, and the broccolini had just the right amount of crunch. We sat across from each other at my small dining table, eating and talking about everything, work, Saviour's party, our upcoming trip, random memories from our childhoods.

"Oh, this is good as fuck," Tool said, licking his fingers as he sat back from his plate.

I was all smiles. I wasn't nervous about the food because one thing I could do was throw down. Oxtails were my only challenge in the kitchen, but everything else? I had that shit on lock.

After we finished eating, we sat in the living room sipping on Taylor Port. The wine was hitting just right, warming me from the inside out. We were both a little tipsy, laughing louder than usual, touching each other more freely.

"This motherfucka strong," Tool said, reading the bottle for the third time like he couldn't believe it.

"Yeah, don't sleep on Tay-Tay," I added, laughing.

I wasn't into wine until I was pregnant with Saviour, but now it was my go-to. And it seemed like I'd put Tool onto something new too. He kept refilling our glasses, and I wasn't mad at it.

When I finished the dishes, he offered to help, but I told him to relax. We cuddled up on the couch and put on a movie some action film he'd been wanting to see. But about an hour in, the movie started watching us because we were too wrapped up in each other. His arms were around me, my head on his chest. Everything about this felt right.

"You know you different, right?" Tool said suddenly, his voice low and serious.

I lifted my head to look at him. "Different how?"

"Different like . . . I ain't never had this before. This peace. This ease. I can just . . . be. You feel me?"

I nodded, my throat getting tight. "I feel you. You're different too."

"Nah, for real though," he continued, sitting up a little so he could look me in the eyes. "I know you been through some shit. I know that nigga put you through hell. But I want you to know I see you. Not just the pretty face, the good-ass cooking, or the way you look in that robe." He smirked, and I playfully hit his chest.

"I see you, Kia. The woman who finally said enough is enough and filed them papers. The woman who's out here raising a whole son and still managing to smile. The woman who's scared to let somebody love her because she's been hurt too many times. I see all that, and I'm telling you right now, I ain't going nowhere."

Tears pricked at my eyes, and I tried to blink them away, but one escaped down my cheek. Tool wiped it away with his thumb.

"Don't cry, baby. I got you. I promise I got you."

"I know," I whispered. "I'm just . . . I'm not used to this."

"Get used to it," he said, pulling me back into his chest. "Because this is what we doing now. This is us."

I closed my eyes and let myself sink into him, into this moment, into the possibility of something real. For so long, I'd been running from my past, from pain, from the idea that I could ever have something good again. But here, wrapped up in Tool's arms, in my own house, with my divorce papers finally filed, I realized I didn't have to run anymore.

I was home.

***

Tool's hands moved from my back to my waist, his touch more intentional now.

"Kia," he said, my name coming out thick with want.

I looked up at him, and the way he was staring at me made my whole body heat up. This wasn't like before. This time, there were no boundaries. No "I don't fuck with married women." The papers were filed. I was on my way to being free. And he knew it.

"Yeah?" I whispered.

Instead of answering, he kissed me. Not the gentle, sweet kisses we'd been sharing. This was different, hungry, like he'd been holding back for months and couldn't anymore. His hands gripped my waist tighter, pulling me onto his lap so I was straddling him on the couch.

I felt him beneath me, hard and ready. The Taylor Port had me feeling loose. I rolled my hips against him, and he groaned into my mouth.

"Fuck, Kia," he breathed, breaking the kiss to look at me with those intense eyes. "You sure about this?"

I nodded, biting my lip. "I'm sure."

That was all he needed. He stood up, effortlessly lifting me with him, my legs wrapped around his waist as he carried me upstairs to my bedroom. He laid me down on the bed gently, like I was something precious.

The silk scarf came off first, then my robe, leaving me in nothing but my bare skin. Tool stood at the edge of the bed, taking me in, his eyes roaming over every inch of me.

"Damn, baby," he said, his voice barely above a whisper. "You're perfect."

I watched as he pulled his shirt over his head, revealing the body I'd only felt through his clothes before broad shoulders, defined chest, abs. Then came his gym shorts, his boxers, and finally, all of him. And Lord have mercy, this man was blessed.

He climbed onto the bed, hovering over me, his weight supported by his arms as he kissed me again. Slower this time. Savoring it. His lips moved from my mouth to my neck, to my collarbone, down to my breasts. He took his time, paying attention to every reaction, every sound I made, every shiver that ran through my body.

"Tool," I breathed, arching into him.

"I got you, baby," he said against my skin. "I'ma take care of you."

And he did. He kissed his way down my body, his hands exploring, caressing, his touch setting me on fire. When he finally settled between my thighs, I gasped, my hands gripping the sheets as he put his mouth to work.

It felt better than the first time. Sacavè never put in this kind of effort. Never made me feel like my pleasure mattered. But Tool? Tool was different. He took his time, listening to my body, adjusting to what I needed, what I wanted. His tongue moved with purpose, his fingers joining in, and I couldn't hold back the moans escaping my lips.

"Oh my God," I moaned, my back arching off the bed as the pressure built. "Tool, I—"

"Let it go, baby," he said, his voice sending vibrations through me. "I got you."

And I did. I let go, my body trembling. My thighs shook, my toes curled, and I called out his name like a prayer. He didn't stop until every last aftershock had run through my body.

When he finally came up for air, his lips glistening with my juices, he looked at me with a satisfied smirk. "That's just the beginning."

He reached over to his bag on the floor, pulling out a condom from his wallet. I watched as he rolled it on, then positioned himself between my legs, his eyes locked on mine.

"You ready?" he asked.

"Yeah," I whispered.

He entered me slowly, giving me time to adjust. And God, the way he filled me up it was perfect. Like our bodies were made for each other. He started moving, his strokes deep and deliberate, each one hitting spots that made me see stars.

"Fuck, Kia," he groaned, his forehead pressed against mine. "You feel so good, baby."

I wrapped my legs around his waist, pulling him deeper, matching his rhythm. Our bodies moved together like we'd done this a thousand times before. He whispered in my ear, telling me how beautiful I was, how good I felt, how long he'd been waiting for this moment.

"Right there," I gasped as he hit that perfect spot. "Right there."

"Right there?" he asked, his pace quickening. "Then cum for me."

And I did. My second orgasm hit me even harder than the first, my nails digging into his back as I cried out. Feeling me tighten around him pushed Tool over the edge, and he buried his face in my neck as he reached his own release.

We stayed like that for a minute, both of us catching our breath. He kissed my forehead, my cheeks, my lips.

"That was . . ." I started, but couldn't find the words.

"I know," he said, smiling down at me. "I know."

He pulled out carefully, disposed of the condom, then came back to bed and pulled me into his arms. I rested my head on his chest.

"No regrets?" he asked softly.

"None," I said, meaning it with my whole heart. "You?"

"Baby, the only thing I regret is not doing this sooner," he said, kissing the top of my head.

We lay there in comfortable silence, our legs tangled together, his fingers drawing lazy circles on my back. This was what I'd been missing. This intimacy. This connection. This feeling of being completely safe and satisfied in someone's arms.

"Kia?" Tool said after a while.

"Yeah?"

"I meant what I said earlier. I ain't going nowhere. This is real for me."

I lifted my head to look at him, seeing nothing but sincerity in his eyes. "It's real for me too."

He kissed me again, and I knew in that moment that this was just the beginning of something beautiful.

Before we eventually fell asleep wrapped in each other's arms, completely content, I heard his voice.

"You good?" he mumbled into my hair.

"Yeah," I whispered. "I'm good."

And for the first time in a long time, I really was.

***

The next morning, I woke up to the smell of coffee. I stretched and realized Tool wasn't in bed. I threw on my robe and padded downstairs to find him in the kitchen, moving around like he'd been there a hundred times before.

"Morning, beautiful," he said, handing me a cup of coffee, fixed just the way I liked it light and sweet with two pumps of caramel syrup.

"Good morning," I said, taking a sip. "You didn't have to do this."

"I know. But I wanted to. Plus, you cooked last night, so it's only right."

I smiled, leaning against the counter and watching him. He was making breakfast: scrambled eggs with cheese, turkey bacon, and toast. Simple, but the fact that he was even doing it made my heart swell.

"What you wanna do today?" he asked, flipping the bacon.

"I don't know. I just wanna be with you. We could stay in, watch movies, chill. Or we could go out. I'm down for whatever."

"Bet. Let's just vibe then. We got the whole weekend."

***

And we did. We spent Saturday doing absolutely nothing and everything at the same time. We watched movies, a romantic comedy that made me cry, an action thriller that had Tool's anxiety on ten. We talked about life, our childhoods, our dreams, our fears. We laughed about stupid shit like the time I accidentally put salt instead of sugar in my coffee and didn't realize it until I was halfway through the cup, or the time Tool got pulled over for speeding and tried to convince the cop he was rushing to the hospital for a family emergency.

We ordered takeout from this Thai place I'd been wanting to try, even though we had leftovers from last night. The pad Thai was sooo good, the spring rolls were crispy and fresh, and we ate it straight out of the containers.

At one point, Tool got up and started going through my vinyl collection, something I'd been building since I moved into this house. He pulled out an old Anita Baker album and put it on the turntable.

"You like Anita?" he asked, surprised.

"Of course. My mama used to play her all the time when I was growing up," I said.

He came back to the couch and pulled me into his arms as "Sweet Love" filled the room. We rocked together, not really dancing, just existing in the moment.

***

That night, as we lay in bed, Tool turned to me. "You know what's crazy?"

"What?"

"I feel like I been knowing you forever. Like we been doing this."

"I feel the same way," I admitted. "It's wild because it hasn't even been that long, but it just... fits."

"That's how you know it's real," he said, kissing my forehead. "When it fits, it fits."

I closed my eyes, feeling more at peace than I had in years.

***

Sunday morning came too fast. Tool had to head back to his place to get ready for work the next day, and I had to pick up Saviour from Sacavè.

"I don't wanna leave," Tool said, wrapping his arms around me at the door.

"I don't want you to leave either," I said, resting my head on his chest.

"Next time, you coming to my spot," he said.

"Okay."

He kissed me one more time, then grabbed his bag and headed out. I watched him pull out of the driveway, feeling both sad and full at the same time.

***

A couple of hours later, I pulled up to Sacavè's house to get Saviour. I texted him when I got there, but he didn't respond. A few minutes later, he came outside with Saviour, who ran straight to the car.

"Hey, baby!" I said, hugging him tight.

"Hey, Ma! Daddy said I could get a dog!" Saviour said excitedly, his eyes wide with hope.

"We'll see," I said, laughing. That was parent code for "probably not, but I don't want to crush your dreams right now."

Sacavè walked up to the car, and I could tell something was off. He looked tired. Stressed. Like he had something heavy on his mind and it was weighing him down.

"We need to talk," he said.

"About what?" I asked, already knowing where this was going.

"About them papers," he said. "I never signed that shit, Kia. Somebody forged my signature."

I stared at him, genuinely confused. "Sacavè, I don't know what you talking about. I gave you the papers months ago."

"And I'm saying I ain't sign it. Who did?" he asked.

"I don't know! But it wasn't me. My attorney filed what they had. If your signature is on there and you didn't sign it, then you need to figure out who did. But don't come at me like I did something wrong."

He stared at me for a long moment.

"A'ight. We'll see."

He walked back into the house without another word, and I drove off, my mind racing. Who the fuck would forge his signature? And why?

But then it hit me.

Sena.

It had to be. She was the only one who had access to his stuff, his life. She was the one who answered his phone that night I called. The one who'd been playing house with my family for years.

I looked in the rearview mirror at Saviour, who was playing with his iPad in the backseat, completely oblivious to the adult drama swirling around him. He was happy. I was happy. And in six months, I'd be officially free.

That was all that mattered.

***

Later that night, after I'd put Saviour to bed and done my nightly routine I laid in bed thinking about everything. About Sacavè's accusation. About Sena. About Tool. About the life I was building for myself then my phone buzzed interrupting my thoughts with a text from Tool: *Miss you already. Can't wait for Puerto Rico.*

I smiled, my stomach stomach had those butterflies it always did when I heard from him.

Miss you too. 3 more days, I texted back.

I'm counting, he responded.

I set my phone on the nightstand and stared up at the ceiling. So much had changed in such a short time. Two weeks ago, I was still technically stuck, married on paper, tied to a man who didn't love me the way I deserved. And now? Now I was free. Or at least on my way to freedom.

I thought about what Sacavè said and then what my attorney said about things that could set us back, I even thought about how much love she had to have for this nigga to commit a felony by forging his signature.

Sacavè had that effect on me before so I could only imagine. When I asked her for help, though I was thinking more like influencing him to sign, but a win is a win. I didn't say anything to Sacavè about my theory. Part of me wanted to warn him, to tell him what I suspected about Sena. But another part of me, the petty, hurt part, wanted him to figure it out on his own. To feel the betrayal from someone he trusted. To understand what it felt like to be blindsided by the person closest to you.

Because that's what he did to me. For years.

I closed my eyes and whispered a prayer, something I hadn't done in a while. "God, thank you for getting me through this. Thank you for protecting my peace. Thank you for Tool. Thank you for Saviour. Thank you for giving me the strength to walk away. And whatever happens next…I trust you."

And for the first time in years, I meant it.

TO BE CONTINUED IN BOOK 2…

Lock Down Publications and Ca$h Presents
Assisted Publishing Packages

Due to an increase in the price of services we have increased our prices. The prices below reflect the price increase as of 11/1/24.

BASIC PACKAGE **$699** Editing Cover Design Formatting	**UPGRADED PACKAGE** **$1000** Typing Editing Cover Design Formatting Upload eBooks to Amazon Upload Paperback to Amazon
ADVANCE PACKAGE **$1,400** Typing Editing (line editing/content) Cover Design Formatting Copyright Registration Proofreading Upload eBooks to Amazon Upload Paperback to Amazon	**LDP SUPREME PACKAGE** **$1,700** Typing Editing (line editing/content) Cover Design Formatting Copyright Registration Proofreading Set up Amazon Account Upload eBooks to Amazon Upload Paperback to Amazon Advertise on LDP's Amazon and Facebook Page

***

Other services available upon request.
Additional charges may apply

Lock Down Publications
P.O. Box 944
Stockbridge, GA 30281-9998
Phone: 470 303-9761
Email: lockdownpublications@gmail.com

Submission Guideline

Submit the first three chapters of your completed manuscript to ldpsubmissions@gmail.com. In the subject line add **Your Book's Title**. The manuscript must be in a Word Doc file and sent as an attachment. Document should be in Times New Roman, double spaced, and in size 12 font. Also, provide your synopsis and full contact information. If sending multiple submissions, they must each be in a separate email.

Have a story but no way to send it electronically? You can still submit to LDP/Ca$h Presents. Send in the first three chapters, written or typed, of your completed manuscript to:

LDP: Submissions Dept
P.O. Box 944
Stockbridge, GA 30281-9998

DO NOT send original manuscript. Must be a duplicate.
Provide your synopsis and a cover letter containing your full contact information.

Thanks for considering LDP and Ca$h Presents.

NEW RELEASES

BLOODLINE OF A SAVAGE 1-3
THESE VICIOUS STREETS 1-3
RELENTLESS GOON 1-3
BY PRINCE A. TAUHID

THE BUTTERFLY MAFIA 1-3
BY FUMIYA PAYNE

A THUG'S STREET PRINCESS 1&2
BY MEESHA

CITY OF SMOKE 3
BY MOLOTTI

GET IT IN SLUGS 1 &2
BY B. STALL

STANDING ON HER BUSINESS 1&2
BY DG SANTANA

STEPPERS 1,2&3
THE REAL BADDIES OF CHI-RAQ
BY KING RIO

THE LANE 1&2
BY KEN-KEN SPENCE

THUG OF SPADES 1&2
LOVE IN THE TRENCHES 2
CORNER BOYS
BY COREY ROBINSON

TIL DEATH 3
BY ARYANNA

LOVE ME OR LET ME GO | R. FACEY

THE BIRTH OF A GANGSTER 4
BY DELMONT PLAYER

PRODUCT OF THE STREETS 1-3
BY DEMOND "MONEY" ANDERSON

NO TIME FOR ERROR
BY KEESE

MONEY HUNGRY DEMONS 1-2
BY TRANAY ADAMS

HUB CITY MENACE 1-3
BY J. WHITE

A THUGGISH PASSION 1&2
LAND OF DA HOOLIGANZ 1-4
KILLAZ ON STANDBY 1&2
BY IRA B.

FO'EVA ROLLIN 1&2
BY ASSA RAYMOND BAKER

THE LEVEL UP 1&3
BY LUXURY KING

Coming Soon from Lock Down Publications/Ca$h Presents

IF YOU CROSS ME ONCE 6
ANGEL V
By Anthony Fields

A THUGS STREET PRINCESS 3
By Meesha

CORNER BOYS 2
By Corey Robinson

THA TAKEOVER
By Keith Chandler

BETRAYAL OF A G 2
By Ray Vinci

SAVAGE FAMILY EMPIRE 1&2
SOULLESS GOON 1,2&3
THE DIRTY SIDE OF MONEY 1,2&3
By Prince

FOR MY ENEMY'S SAKE
AMBITIONS OF A SLIDER
FRESH OFF DA PORCH
By IRA B.

BY THE TRUCKLOAD 1-4
TIPPIN' THE SCALES 1-3
BAD BITCHES WIT GUNZ 3
PROBLEM SOLVED 2
By Christopher "Diesel" Hornezes

Available Now

RESTRAINING ORDER 1 & 2
By **CA$H & Coffee**

LOVE KNOWS NO BOUNDARIES 1-3
By **Coffee**

RAISED AS A GOON I, II, III & IV
BRED BY THE SLUMS I, II, III
BLAST FOR ME I & II
ROTTEN TO THE CORE I II III
A BRONX TALE I, II, III
DUFFLE BAG CARTEL I II III IV V VI
HEARTLESS GOON I II III IV V
A SAVAGE DOPEBOY I II
DRUG LORDS I II III
CUTTHROAT MAFIA I II
KING OF THE TRENCHES
By **Ghost**

LAY IT DOWN I & II
LAST OF A DYING BREED I II
BLOOD STAINS OF A SHOTTA I & II III
By **Jamaica**

LOYAL TO THE GAME I II III
LIFE OF SIN I, II III
By **TJ & Jelissa**

IF LOVING HIM IS WRONG…I & II
LOVE ME EVEN WHEN IT HURTS I II III
By **Jelissa**

PUSH IT TO THE LIMIT
By **Bre' Hayes**

LOVE ME OR LET ME GO | R. FACEY

BLOODY COMMAS I & II
SKI MASK CARTEL I, II & III
KING OF NEW YORK I II, III IV V
RISE TO POWER I II III
COKE KINGS I II III IV V
BORN HEARTLESS I II III IV
KING OF THE TRAP I II
By **T.J. Edwards**

WHEN THE STREETS CLAP BACK I & II III
THE HEART OF A SAVAGE I II III IV
MONEY MAFIA I II
LOYAL TO THE SOIL I II III
By **Jibril Williams**

A DISTINGUISHED THUG STOLE MY HEART I II & III
LOVE SHOULDN'T HURT I II III IV
RENEGADE BOYS 1-4
PAID IN KARMA 1-3
SAVAGE STORMS 1-3
AN UNFORESEEN LOVE 1-3
BABY, I'M WINTERTIME COLD 1-3
A THUG'S STREET PRINCESS 1&2
By **Meesha**

A GANGSTER'S CODE 1-3
A GANGSTER'S SYN 1-3
THE SAVAGE LIFE 1-3
CHAINED TO THE STREETS 1-3
BLOOD ON THE MONEY 1-3
A GANGSTA'S PAIN 1-3
BEAUTIFUL LIES AND UGLY TRUTHS
CHURCH IN THESE STREETS
By **J-Blunt**

CUM FOR ME 1-8
An LDP Erotica Collaboration

LOVE ME OR LET ME GO | R. FACEY

BLOOD OF A BOSS 1-5
SHADOWS OF THE GAME
TRAP BASTARD
By **Askari**

THE STREETS BLEED MURDER 1-3
THE HEART OF A GANGSTA 1-3
By **Jerry Jackson**

WHEN A GOOD GIRL GOES BAD
By **Adrienne**

THE COST OF LOYALTY 1-3
By **Kweli**

BRIDE OF A HUSTLA 1-3
THE FETTI GIRLS 1-3
CORRUPTED BY A GANGSTA 1-4
BLINDED BY HIS LOVE
THE PRICE YOU PAY FOR LOVE 1-3
DOPE GIRL MAGIC 1-3
By **Destiny Skai**

A KINGPIN'S AMBITION
A KINGPIN'S AMBITION II
I MURDER FOR THE DOUGH
By **Ambitious**

TRUE SAVAGE 1-7
DOPE BOY MAGIC 1-3
MIDNIGHT CARTEL 1-3
CITY OF KINGZ 1&2
NIGHTMARE ON SILENT AVE
THE PLUG OF LIL MEXICO 1&2
CLASSIC CITY
By **Chris Green**

LOVE ME OR LET ME GO | R. FACEY

A GANGSTER'S REVENGE 1-4
THE BOSS MAN'S DAUGHTERS 1-5
A SAVAGE LOVE 1&2
BAE BELONGS TO ME 1&2
A HUSTLER'S DECEIT 1-3
WHAT BAD BITCHES DO 1-3
SOUL OF A MONSTER 1-3
KILL ZONE
A DOPE BOY'S QUEEN 1-3
TIL DEATH 1-3
IMMA DIE BOUT MINE 1-6
DYING FOR LIKES
By **Aryanna**

A DOPEBOY'S PRAYER
By **Eddie "Wolf" Lee**

THE KING CARTEL 1-3
By **Frank Gresham**

THESE NIGGAS AIN'T LOYAL 1-3
By **Nikki Tee**

GANGSTA SHYT 1-3
By **CATO**

THE ULTIMATE BETRAYAL
By **Phoenix**

BOSS'N UP 1-3
By **Royal Nicole**

I LOVE YOU TO DEATH
By **Destiny J**

I RIDE FOR MY HITTA
I STILL RIDE FOR MY HITTA
By **Misty Holt**

LOVE & CHASIN' PAPER
By **Qay Crockett**

TO DIE IN VAIN
SINS OF A HUSTLA
By **ASAD**

BROOKLYN HUSTLAZ
By **Boogsy Morina**

BROOKLYN ON LOCK 1 & 2
By **Sonovia**

GANGSTA CITY
By **Teddy Duke**

A DRUG KING AND HIS DIAMOND 1-3
A DOPEMAN'S RICHES
HER MAN, MINE'S TOO 1&2
CASH MONEY HO'S
THE WIFEY I USED TO BE 1&2
PRETTY GIRLS DO NASTY THINGS
By **Nicole Goosby**

LIPSTICK KILLAH 1-3
CRIME OF PASSION 1-3
FRIEND OR FOE 1-3
By **Mimi**

TRAPHOUSE KING 1-3
KINGPIN KILLAZ 1-3
STREET KINGS 1&2
PAID IN BLOOD 1&2
CARTEL KILLAZ 1-3
DOPE GODS 1&2
By **Hood Rich**

THE STREETS ARE CALLING
By **Duquie Wilson**

STEADY MOBBN' 1-3
THE STREETS STAINED MY SOUL 1-3
By **Marcellus Allen**

WHO SHOT YA 1-3
SON OF A DOPE FIEND 1-4
HEAVEN GOT A GHETTO 1&2
SKI MASK MONEY 1&2
By **Renta**

GORILLAZ IN THE BAY 1-4
TEARS OF A GANGSTA 1/&2
3X KRAZY 1&2
STRAIGHT BEAST MODE 1&2
By **DE'KARI**

TRIGGADALE 1-3
MURDA WAS THE CASE 1-3
By **Elijah R. Freeman**

SLAUGHTER GANG 1-3
RUTHLESS HEART 1-3
By **Willie Slaughter**

GOD BLESS THE TRAPPERS 1-3
THESE SCANDALOUS STREETS 1-3
FEAR MY GANGSTA 1-5
THESE STREETS DON'T LOVE NOBODY 1-2
BURY ME A G 1-5
A GANGSTA'S EMPIRE 1-4
THE DOPEMAN'S BODYGAURD 1&2
THE REALEST KILLAZ 1-3
THE LAST OF THE OGS 1-3
By **Tranay Adams**

MARRIED TO A BOSS 1-3
By **Destiny Skai & Chris Green**

KINGZ OF THE GAME 1-7
CRIME BOSS 1-4
By **Playa Ray**

FUK SHYT
By **Blakk Diamond**

DON'T F#CK WITH MY HEART 1&2
By **Linnea**

ADDICTED TO THE DRAMA 1-3
IN THE ARM OF HIS BOSS
By **Jamila**

LOYALTY AIN'T PROMISED 1&2
By **Keith Williams**

YAYO 1-4
A SHOOTER'S AMBITION 1&2
BRED IN THE GAME
By **S. Allen**

TRAP GOD 1-3
RICH $AVAGE 1-3
MONEY IN THE GRAVE 1-3
CARTEL MONEY 1&2
By **Martell Troublesome Bolden**

FOREVER GANGSTA 1&2
GLOCKS ON SATIN SHEETS 1&2
By **Adrian Dulan**

TOE TAGZ 1-4
LEVELS TO THIS SHYT 1&2
IT'S JUST ME AND YOU
By **Ah'Million**

KINGPIN DREAMS 1-3
RAN OFF ON DA PLUG
By **Paper Boi Rari**

THE STREETS MADE ME 1-3
By **Larry D. Wright**

CONFESSIONS OF A GANGSTA 1-4
CONFESSIONS OF A JACKBOY 1-3
CONFESSIONS OF A HITMAN
CONFESSIONS OF A DOPE BOY
By **Nicholas Lock**

I'M NOTHING WITHOUT HIS LOVE
SINS OF A THUG
TO THE THUG I LOVED BEFORE
A GANGSTA SAVED XMAS
IN A HUSTLER I TRUST
By **Monet Dragun**

QUIET MONEY 1-3
THUG LIFE 1-3
EXTENDED CLIP 1&2
A GANGSTA'S PARADISE
By **Trai'Quan**

CAUGHT UP IN THE LIFE 1-3
THE STREETS NEVER LET GO 1-3
By **Robert Baptiste**

NEW TO THE GAME 1-3
MONEY, MURDER & MEMORIES 1-3
By **Malik D. Rice**

CREAM 2-3
THE STREETS WILL TALK
By **Yolanda Moore**

THE STREETS WILL NEVER CLOSE 1-3
By **K'ajji**

LIFE OF A SAVAGE 1-4
A GANGSTA'S QUR'AN 1-4
MURDA SEASON 1-3
GANGLAND CARTEL 1-3
CHI'RAQ GANGSTAS 1-4
KILLERS ON ELM STREET 1-3
JACK BOYZ N DA BRONX 1-3
A DOPEBOY'S DREAM 1-3
JACK BOYS VS DOPE BOYS 1-3
COKE GIRLZ
COKE BOYS
SOSA GANG 1&2
BRONX SAVAGES
BODYMORE KINGPINS
BLOOD OF A GOON
By **Romell Tukes**

CONCRETE KILLA 1-3
VICIOUS LOYALTY 1-3
BLOODY MONEY BAGS
By **Kingpen**

THE ULTIMATE SACRIFICE 1-6
KHADIFI
IF YOU CROSS ME ONCE 1-3
ANGEL 1-4
IN THE BLINK OF AN EYE
By **Anthony Fields**

THE LIFE OF A HOOD STAR
By **Ca$h & Rashia Wilson**

NIGHTMARES OF A HUSTLA 1-3
BLOOD AND GAMES 1&2
By **King Dream**

GHOST MOB
By **Stilloan Robinson**

HARD AND RUTHLESS 1&2
MOB TOWN 251
THE BILLIONAIRE BENTLEYS 1-3
REAL G'S MOVE IN SILENCE
By **Von Diesel**

MOB TIES 1-7
SOUL OF A HUSTLER, HEART OF A KILLER 1-3
GORILLAZ IN THE TRENCHES
OOPS CRY TOO 1&2
THE DAUGHTER OF A CARTEL BOSS
By **SayNoMore**

BODYMORE MURDERLAND 1-3
THE BIRTH OF A GANGSTER 1-4
By **Delmont Player**

FOR THE LOVE OF A BOSS 1&2
By **C. D. Blue**

KILLA KOUNTY 1-5
TENDER
By **Khufu**

MOBBED UP 1-4
THE BRICK MAN 1-5
THE COCAINE PRINCESS 1-10
STEPPERS 1-3
SUPER GREMLIN 1-4
A GANGSTA'S SON
By **King Rio**

MONEY GAME 1&2
By **Smoove Dolla**

A GANGSTA'S KARMA 1-5
By **FLAME**

KING OF THE TRENCHES 1-3
By **GHOST & TRANAY ADAMS**

BAD BITCHES WIT GUNZ 1&2
PROBLEM SOLVED
By **"Christopher Diesel" Hornezes**

QUEEN OF THE ZOO 1&2
By **Black Migo**

GRIMEY WAYS 1-3
BETRAYAL OF A G
By **Ray Vinci**

XMAS WITH AN ATL SHOOTER
By **Ca$h & Destiny Skai**

KING KILLA 1&2
By **Vincent "Vitto" Holloway**

BETRAYAL OF A THUG 1&2
By **Fre$h**

COUNTDOWN OF A KILLA 1&2
SEX, MURDER AND GOD 1&2
GUNS DOWN, BOTTOMS UP 1&2
By Lo-Life

THE MURDER QUEENS 1-7
By **Michael Gallon**

FOR THE LOVE OF BLOOD 1-4
By **Jamel Mitchell**

LOVE ME OR LET ME GO | R. FACEY

HOOD CONSIGLIERE 1&2
NO TIME FOR ERROR
By **Keese**

PROTÉGÉ OF A LEGEND 1,2&3
LOVE IN THE TRENCHES 1&2
By **Corey Robinson**

THE PLUG'S RUTHLESS DAUGHTER 1&2
By **Tony Daniels**

BORN IN THE GRAVE 1-3
CRIME PAYS
By **Self Made Tay**

MOAN IN MY MOUTH
By **XTASY**

TORN BETWEEN A GANGSTER AND A GENTLEMAN
By **J-BLUNT & Miss Kim**

LOYALTY IS EVERYTHING 1-3
CITY OF SMOKE 1-3
By **Molotti**

HERE TODAY GONE TOMORROW 1&2
By **Fly Rock**

WOMEN LIE MEN LIE 1-4
FIFTY SHADES OF SNOW 1-3
STACK BEFORE YOU SPLURGE
GIRLS FALL LIKE DOMINOES
NAÏVE TO THE STREETS
By **ROY MILLIGAN**

PILLOW PRINCESS
By **S. Hawkins**

LOVE ME OR LET ME GO | R. FACEY

THE BUTTERFLY MAFIA 1-3
SALUTE MY SAVAGERY 1&2
By **Fumiya Payne**

THE LANE 1&2
By Ken-Ken Spence

THE PUSSY TRAP 1-5
By **Nene Capri**

DIRTY DNA
By **Blaque**

SANCTIFIED AND HORNY
by **XTASY**

BOOKS BY LDP'S CEO, CA$H

TRUST IN NO MAN
TRUST IN NO MAN 2
TRUST IN NO MAN 3
BONDED BY BLOOD
SHORTY GOT A THUG
THUGS CRY
THUGS CRY 2
THUGS CRY 3
TRUST NO BITCH
TRUST NO BITCH 2
TRUST NO BITCH 3
TIL MY CASKET DROPS
RESTRAINING ORDER
RESTRAINING ORDER 2
IN LOVE WITH A CONVICT
LIFE OF A HOOD STAR
XMAS WITH AN ATL SHOOTER

www.ingramcontent.com/pod-product-compliance
Lightning Source LLC
Chambersburg PA
CBHW070445260626
47161CB00004B/1210